KING ROOSTER

King
Rooster

by Leo R. Ellis

Funk & Wagnalls Company, Inc.   *New York*

1

To Margaret
whose faith, belief, and understanding
are far beyond my own understanding.

KING ROOSTER

CHAPTER 1

Phil Martinson entered the office of the Kendall Photo Studio and dropped the heavy press camera case against the wall. "Weddings," he said to the empty office, "this town is fraught with weddings."

A round-faced young man with a straw-colored crew cut poked his head through the open front door. "What gives with weddings?" he said. "You getting married or something?"

"I'm not getting married, or nothing. But I've been to so many weddings lately, I could do the groom's, the bride's, and the minister's part without muffing a line. Come on in, Bimbo," Phil added. "And close the door."

Bimbo Barnes was inches shorter than Phil Martinson, and where Phil was long-muscled and slim, Bimbo was rotund and pudgy. "Scotty send you out to take pictures of another wedding?" he asked cheerfully.

Phil groaned. "What else?"

"You do other things," Bimbo said, dropping into a chair. "Yesterday he sent you out to shoot a kids' party."

"That was worse. At least at a wedding the guests don't kick the photographer in the shins." Phil opened the camera case and took out four film holders. He had been a shutterbug ever since he was old enough to hold a camera, and after his graduation from high school in June, he had gone to work for Scotty Kendall.

"I don't know what else you expected on this job," Bimbo said.

"I expected something more exciting than weddings."

"Excitement? In Seacrest? Har-de-har-har."

Phil knew there was little in the excitement line around the little city of Seacrest, but he had hoped to be in on the ground floor if anything did happen. Nothing had happened now in almost two months, and Phil was downright disappointed. He was beginning to feel he could have done something better with his vacation before going away to college. "Scotty probably wouldn't let me handle a big job anyway," he said. "He'd be on the spot with a camera, and I'd be out somewhere shooting a garden party, or a . . . a wedding."

Phil had a great deal of respect for Scotty Kendall as a photographer. That was why he had been so anxious to come to work for him. Scotty's place was not only a regular photo studio; Scotty also did commercial work for large concerns. At one time he had been a news photographer, and he still sold news shots and feature spreads, free lance. But Scotty had explained to Phil that the routine assignments were the bread and butter of his business.

"It's the weddings that pay your salary," Bimbo said.

Phil carried the film holders into the darkroom and banged them down on the work table. Scotty was a stickler for rules. Rule number one on his list was that a good photographer was never caught without fresh film ready to slip into his camera. Phil spread the holders out and reached up on the shelf for the box of cut film as Bimbo entered. "Snap off the light," he said. "I'll have to develop this stuff and load the holders, or Scotty will blow a gasket."

Bimbo groped his way to the table in the blackness. "I wouldn't have stopped by if I'd known you were going to work," he said. "I thought maybe we could go over to the malt shop."

"Things around here are done by the numbers." Expertly, Phil's fingers worked in the darkness, slipping the exposed film out of the holders and into the metal hangers. By the numbers, he thought. Scotty had typed up a list of rules a photographer should follow, and they had been numbered from one to ten. Scotty had even made Phil tape the list to the dash of his car. "By the numbers," Phil said aloud as he carried the hangers over to the developing tank. "Hep-two-three-four."

"You won't have to worry about that much longer," Bimbo said. "It won't be long now until we'll be going down to Los Angeles to get our classes lined up for school."

Phil nodded in the darkness. He and Bimbo Barnes had been together ever since their grade school days, and they were going to stick together through college. In high school Phil had been a track letterman, while Bimbo had been equipment manager for the team. It was only natural that they had applied for entrance at the same college, and now both of them had been accepted.

"I may get a chance to do some real photography down there," Phil said, dropping the hangers into the tank. "At least I'm going out for the school paper, and I might get on as a stringer for one of the metropolitan dailies."

"We'll have a swell time down there, all right. If I had to try it alone, I don't think I'd go."

Phil agitated the hangers in the developing fluid a few times to make sure that the air bubbles had been knocked off, then rinsed his hands under the tap and dried them before he went back to handle the fresh film. "I wish you'd learn to load this stuff, Bimbo. It's simple enough for you to understand. Now listen and I'll tell you what I'm doing."

"You sound like my father."

Carefully, Phil explained each step as he performed the act. "When you have the film set in the holder, you slip this sheet of plastic into the groove over the film. That's called a dark slide, and it keeps the light from reaching the sensitized surface of the film."

"When are you going to be through there? I'm hungry."

"Get out of here," Phil said and finished the loading job alone. He had just picked up the holders and snapped on the light when the phone rang.

Out in the office, Bimbo answered the phone. "Kendall's Photo Studio," he said. "We specialize in shooting snappy snapshots."

Phil dropped the holders on the desk and grabbed the telephone. "Knock it off," he hissed. "Good morning," he said into the telephone. "May I help you?"

The voice identified himself as Pete, of the Seacrest Ambulance Service. Phil knew Scotty had a working agreement with the ambulance company to notify him when they received any special calls. "Scotty isn't in," he said. "I'm his assistant. Would you give me the message?"

"OK," Pete said. "We had an emergency call to go out on

Ramona Road, about a mile beyond the high school. A new building fell down or something."

Phil replaced the telephone. He stared at the wall as a slow grin spread across his face. "Man," he said in an awed tone, "this could be my big chance." Quickly he explained the telephone call to Bimbo. "You stay here and answer the phone. I'm on my way out to Ramona Road." He tossed the holders into the camera case and closed the lid. "Oh, yes. When that timer bell rings, dunk those hangers into the hypo."

"But . . ."

Phil waved Bimbo's protest away. "They're only wedding pictures," he said.

"But hadn't you ought to tell Scotty about that call?"

"He's clear out at the Topmost Dairy, shooting a job out there."

"That's only a mile out of town," Bimbo said.

"Look," Phil said impatiently, "why do you keep throwing up roadblocks? Don't you think I can handle this job alone?"

"Sure . . . I think so . . . maybe . . . but . . ." Bimbo stopped when he saw he was talking to a closed door.

Phil put the camera case into the back of his old car, jumped in and, after a sweeping U turn, headed for Ramona Road. He caught himself banging on the steering wheel and straightened up to drive more sedately, fighting down his impatience to get out to the scene of the accident. He didn't want people to think he was a kid on his first job. A professional news cameraman was blasé about these things; even a major disaster couldn't shake them. That was the way he was going to act, he wasn't going to panic. Why should he panic? He'd been through all this a hundred times before—in his mind.

Phil had his own personal 35mm camera, but Scotty insisted he use the larger, and more complex, press camera. Phil wasn't going to let that bother him—he could handle it as well as any camera, and besides, it made him look more professional.

As he passed the high school buildings, he scarcely glanced at them. They were a part of his past, something he had known a long time ago.

He stepped down hard on the gas when the traffic strung out on Ramona Road. A mile beyond the school, Pete had said. From now on there would be the new electronic plants and the machine shops and engineering offices that had been built in the past few years. In between those would be sprinkled the honky-tonk joints that had sprung up at about the same time.

Impatiently, Phil swung out to pass a slow-moving car, then cut back in again. Almost immediately, he heard the whine of a siren and looked out. Running beside him was a motorcycle cop waving him to pull over. "Oh, no," Phil groaned, "not now." His first impulse was to tromp down, try to outrun the cycle to the building, and then explain. Instead, he stuck his head out of the window. "I'm a news photographer," he shouted. "There's been a bad accident down the road."

It was as if he had spoken some magic phrase. The officer nodded, kicked down on his siren, and roared ahead. Phil got the message fast. He gave his old car the gun, to try and hang on to the officer's tail. "Police escort!" he yelled. "Man, this is really living."

Phil spotted the building when he saw the ambulance standing in front of it. The officer pulled on beyond the driveway to allow Phil to swing into the open dirt area before the newly constructed building. Phil stopped his car in a cloud of dust as he looked around to see if the photographer from the newspaper had beaten him there. Besides the ambulance, there were only a few workmen's cars parked over to one side. He had scooped the opposition.

Phil pulled out the camera and electronic flash gun. He silently thanked Scotty's foresight as he stuffed his jacket pockets with film holders and slid out of the car. He flipped the camera open and fastened on the flash gun as he ran.

Phil was at the rear of the ambulance when he saw two attendants approaching with a loaded stretcher. "Hold it!" he shouted and raised his camera.

The stretcher bearers obeyed. Phil got his first shot. He would need a close-up, so he moved up to the side of the stretcher. He had the camera up to eye level when he froze. He stared down at the stretcher and a sickening sensation hit him in the pit of the stomach.

Phil knew the man. It was Victor Sanchez, an old friend of his. Victor was a construction laborer who had worked for Phil's father for many years. As a little kid, when Phil had gone out on jobs his father's construction company was doing, Victor Sanchez would watch over him. The man had taught Phil how to saw a board in two and how to nail the pieces together. It seemed to Phil that he had known Victor all his life.

The stretcher bearers moved on and hoisted the stretcher into the ambulance. Phil had one foot on the step of the ambulance when he stopped. He wasn't acting like a professional photographer; a professional would stay on the job and get his pictures. Phil brushed at his eyes with the back of his hand and turned to the building.

The ambulance had pulled away before Phil realized he had failed to get the important close-up of the victim.

The building was still only four walls and a roof. There were no doors or windows installed, and as Phil stepped into the front opening, he saw that it was an empty concrete shell. The rafters were one long span from wall to wall. Three of those walls were intact, but the fourth wall had partially collapsed. The concrete had fallen inward, dragging the wooden beams down to make a jumbled mass of broken cement and twisted timbers. Workmen swarmed over the debris.

Phil forced the sight of Victor Sanchez out of his mind and studied the scene before him. Then he took a long shot of the whole thing before he moved closer. For the next few minutes he climbed over the pile, taking pictures, while the jagged concrete and splintered wood tore at his clothes.

He knelt down to take low angle shots for a dramatic effect. He climbed to the top of the rubble to shoot from above. He took pictures of workmen swinging sledges and of workmen straining on pry bars, but after each shot he was plagued by a feeling of dissatisfaction. He had burned up a lot of film, but he still didn't have much—he didn't have anything that anyone else with a camera couldn't take.

When the prints were made, they would show nothing but a group of workmen toiling on a crushed pile of concrete.

Phil checked his film. He had brought the four holders he had loaded, as well as two spares that were in the case. Each holder held two sheets of film, and as Phil had taken each picture, he had reversed the dark slide so the black painted edge was out. This indicated that the film had been exposed, and now he had only one slide that didn't show a black edge.

With only one more shot left, Phil was grimly determined to make that last one count. He had always dreamed of coming up on his first job with one dramatic news shot that would sell to the wire services. Now he had been so anxious that he had wasted most of his film. He had even missed the chance of getting a picture of Victor on the stretcher. A close-up of the victim might have sold, but he had flubbed that when he had let his personal feelings take over.

With a determination to hoard his last piece of film, Phil walked around the spot where the workmen were, to the other side. There was no one around here, and he started to move on when he spotted a small opening in the pile at the floor level. A wooden timber had fallen at an angle, so it held up the concrete to form a tunnel. Phil knelt down to peer in. It was black in there, and not much chance that there was anything inside anyway.

Phil hesitated. If he didn't try something desperate, he might as well take his last routine shot and go back to the studio.

He made a quick decision, got down on his hands and knees, and pushed his camera equipment into the opening before him. The light was blocked out almost immediately, and he was forced to crawl over chunks and feel his way along the crooked crevice. The jagged edges and splintered ends tore at his flesh, and the cement dust sifted down to choke him. He realized he should have taken off his jacket, but it was too late now. If he ever got outside again, he wouldn't be fool enough to crawl back in.

Working his way along, Phil tried not to think of the tons of weight balanced perilously overhead, where a shift could bring the whole thing down to crush him.

It seemed to Phil that he must be near the center of the heap when the tunnel ended abruptly. Running his hand across the obstruction, he found a heavy beam had lodged crossways, blocking his path completely. There was nothing to do now but to back out. He had done nothing but waste precious time; the idea had been a bust.

Phil ran his fingers up the timber to the top and found a foot of empty space between it and the concrete above. He worked himself to his knees and raised as high as he could, with the electronic flash gun held beside his face. He fixed his eyes on the black space beyond the timber and hit the flash button.

The brilliant flash of the gun was gone almost instantaneously, but an image remained fixed on Phil's eyes. The image was a picture of a man lying on the floor, his eyes closed. The man was trapped under the rubble.

"Hello there," Phil called over the timber. "Can you hear me?" The only sound was the beating of his own heart and his own rapid breathing. He forced himself to be calm as he set up his camera for action. He adjusted the focus and diaphragm stop by feel. "Take it easy, boy," he told himself, "this is your big chance."

He poked the camera up over the edge of the beam, so that the flash gun touched the concrete above. He felt the rim of the lens to make sure it was in the clear. Everything had to be perfect now—this was his last film. Slowly he took a deep breath and held it to keep the camera steady, then snapped the picture.

The gun flashed. The shutter clicked and Phil let his breath out all at once. "I got it," he said softly. "I got it."

Phil dragged his camera equipment out and went to look for the foreman of the crew. At first the big man refused to listen, but finally he agreed to come down and look at the opening. As they stood on the floor beside the tunnel, Phil pointed out the spot near the center of the heap. "I think the man's trapped under there," he said.

The foreman studied the spot where Phil had pointed and wiped the sweat from his face. "How do you know he's there?" the man asked gruffly. "Did you see him?"

"I told you I saw him. I crawled back in there through that opening, and I saw him. I couldn't get to him because there was a timber blocking my way."

The foreman studied the opening. "How come you'd crawl into a thing like that in the first place?" he asked suspiciously.

"I'm a news photographer." Phil held up his camera.

The foreman looked at the camera, then looked at Phil. "You may be what you say you are," he said dubiously, "but in my book, you're nuts."

"You mean you're not even going to look for the man?"

"I've got to. It's all I can do. We'll have to bring in a crane to get down through that mess," he said thoughtfully. "If you're lying to me, kid, I'll look you up and break your neck."

Phil felt a sense of elation when he walked around and saw a man with a camera in his hand hurrying through the opening where the door would be. It was the photographer from the *Seacrest Journal*, but that no longer bothered Phil. The press photographer could duplicate most of the other shots, but Phil had one on film that the *Journal* wouldn't get without paying for it.

Scotty had often told him to get something different from the shots taken by the competition. "Look around for a shot that's different," Scotty had said. "Get something they've missed. You'll never sell anything by shooting the same thing."

OK, I've got something different, Phil thought. I took a chance and now I've got something that will sell—it could even rate Phil Martinson a by-line on his very first assignment.

Phil had his camera case in the car when the white station wagon pulled in and stopped. A ruddy-faced, compact little man got out and looked over at Phil. Phil took his time as he sauntered over to his boss.

"What happened here?" Scotty Kendall asked.

Phil managed to keep his voice calm as he explained about the accident. "There's still a man trapped under the debris," he said. "They've sent for a crane to try and get him out."

Scotty's bushy white eyebrows bunched over his blue eyes

as he peered at Phil. "Did you get pictures of everything so far?" he said.

Phil hesitated. He hadn't told Scotty about the missed shot of Victor Sanchez. "I crawled under that heap and got a picture of the man trapped down there," he said.

Scotty regarded him steadily. "Good work, boy," he said. "I hope you remembered everything I've told you."

"Sure, I remembered it like a book. I tell you this shot I took is bound to sell . . ." Phil stopped and snapped his fingers. "But I'd better get it developed and printed. A good news shot sells only when it's hot."

Scotty ran his fingers through his thatch of white hair and grinned. "That sounds familiar," he said. "You get on back. I'll handle the rescue operation." He walked back to the rear of the station wagon.

Phil chuckled to himself as he climbed into his own car. Scotty would do a good job, but he couldn't imagine the little man crawling under that rubble for a picture. He looked down at the list of ten rules taped to the dash. "I won't be needing you anymore," he said aloud. "Today, I'm a professional."

Bimbo was waiting in the office and demanded all the details of the accident. "Was your dad out there?" he asked.

Phil looked puzzled. "I didn't see him. Why?"

"He's the city engineer. I figured he'd be one of the first guys out there if a building fell down."

A worry line appeared between Phil's eyebrows. "Maybe nobody's notified him yet," he said and shrugged off the idea of calling his father. It was more important that he get his films developed right now.

Bimbo stayed close beside Phil in the darkness as he removed the films from the holders and put them into the hangers. Phil agitated them carefully and often. These films were to get special treatment. He didn't want anything to go wrong now. When the timer bell rang, he transferred them to the hypo solution and waited impatiently for them to clear before he turned on the light.

"Now I'll show you what I got," he told Bimbo. He started at one end of the tank and held each dripping negative up to inspect it against the light. "The exposure is right on the nose," he said thoughtfully. "Contrast is good, and the highlights aren't blocked up."

"But how are the pictures?"

"Routine stuff so far," Phil said patiently. He looked at each in turn, then replaced it in the hypo. Before he lifted the last hanger, he closed his eyes. He held the final negative up, opened his eyes, and groaned.

"What's the matter?" Bimbo asked, pushing up to see.

Phil stared at the film, dumbfounded. "It's blank," he said.

"I'll say it's blank," Bimbo said. "Man, that looks like nothing but a pane of glass."

"There's nothing on it."

"That's what I said."

Phil dropped the hanger back into the tank. "Brother," he groaned.

"What happened? Didn't the shutter go off?"

Mechanically, Phil rinsed off his hands and wiped them dry. "The shutter went off," he said miserably. "I heard it."

"Maybe the gun didn't flash."

"The gun flashed." Slowly Phil trudged out into the office and dropped into the chair behind Scotty's desk.

Bimbo followed him out. "What happened then? Why didn't you get a picture?"

Phil sat slumped low in the chair, his chin resting on his breastbone. "I forgot to pull the dark slide," he muttered.

Bimbo stared at him. "You forgot to . . ." He opened and closed his mouth. "Haven't you told me that's the last thing you do before you shoot a picture?"

Phil grunted an answer without looking up.

"And isn't that one of the rules Scotty typed up and had you tape on your dash?"

"It was rule number ten."

"Man." Bimbo made an elaborate motion of wiping sweat from his brow and backed toward the front door. "Nice to have known you," he said. "But I think I'd better go."

CHAPTER 2

THE PRETTY, dark-haired girl behind the fountain in the malt shop looked up as Phil and Bimbo entered. She smiled at Phil and looked at Bimbo. "Business is picking up," she said. "Here comes the calorie buster."

"Hi, Gracie," Bimbo said amiably. He stopped and studied the list of drinks on the wall.

"You know that menu by heart," Gracie said, reaching for a large container. "What will it be, the same?"

"Bring me a root beer," Phil said and started back to a booth.

"I think I'll have . . ." Bimbo said slowly.

". . . a jumbo, double thick choc malt," Gracie said as she scooped up the ice cream.

Bimbo gave her a hurt expression. "You forgot the whipped cream," he said.

Bimbo grunted as he slid into the booth across the table from Phil. "You should have ordered something besides a root beer," he said. "You've had a bad day, boy. You need nourishment."

"I'm not hungry." Phil took a paper napkin and spread it out on the table.

"What's that got to do with it? When I'm down, a little food picks me up."

"I thought your mother put you on a diet."

"She did," Bimbo said, grinning. "I start tomorrow."

"That's what you said yesterday."

"I'm a consistent guy," Bimbo said solemnly. "I'm always going to start tomorrow."

Phil studied the napkin, which he was now folding into small squares. He knew Bimbo was doing his best to cheer him up, but it wasn't having much effect. What had happened out at the building accident that morning was still too much of a crusher. "You're a comic," he said without looking up.

Bimbo leaned over the table. "What did Scotty say when you told him about forgetting to pull the dark slide?"

Phil sighed. "Not much," he said. Phil didn't want to talk about what had happened. It had been such a blow to his pride that he would rather bury the whole thing and try to forget. He looked up and saw Bimbo's disappointed expression. Phil felt guilty—it was a dirty trick to shut old Bimbo out. "Scotty just stood there with those eyes of his boring a couple of holes through me," he said slowly. "Then he said I wasn't the first photographer who had forgotten to pull the dark slide on an important job."

"Didn't he chew you out about forgetting the rules?"

"He didn't have to," Phil said soberly. "He knew I was bleeding."

"You got off plenty easy. If I'd pulled a trick like that, my father would have given me a half hour's lecture on the irresponsibility of modern youth." He looked up as Gracie approached with a tray. "So much for frivolity," he said. "Now let's get down to something serious. Here come the eats."

Phil studied the frosted outside of the mug on the table before him. "Of all the tough breaks," he said. "Right when I had things handed to me on a silver platter."

"Yeah," Bimbo said, picking up a long-handled spoon. "It was a tough break, all right."

"No," Phil said soberly, "it wasn't just a tough break—it was my own fault. I had everything handed to me all right, but I goofed. There's no use trying to kid myself. It was my own fault; I can't blame anyone else."

Bimbo swallowed hard and licked his lips. "I suppose so," he said, "if you want to look at it that way."

"You can't look at it any other way." Phil thoughtfully turned the mug around on the table.

"Oh, I don't know. I heard they saved that guy who was buried under the pile of concrete. If you hadn't found him and told them where to dig, he might have died down there."

Phil snorted. "Big-time hero stuff," he said sarcastically. "You know I didn't crawl in there to save anybody. I went in after a picture."

"OK, have it your own way. But you sure make it tough to cheer you up when you're so technical about details."

Phil pinched the paper napkin into a tight ball and rolled it under his palm on the table. The other workman had been saved, but how about Victor Sanchez? Phil had called the hospital before he left the studio, but they had given him no information on Victor's condition. Phil felt ashamed of himself when he remembered how he had thought he was the only one who'd had a tough break that morning. How about poor Victor? He was a kind, friendly guy whom everybody in town knew and liked. He had really been struck down, and it hadn't been his fault.

Bimbo made a loud sucking sound with his straw at the bottom of his glass. He leaned back and rubbed his stomach. "The end," he said, grinning.

Phil was still deep in his own thoughts. "I wonder how a thing like that could have happened?" he said aloud.

"What happened?"

"That wall collapsing like that."

"I don't know," Bimbo said, "but it will put your dad on the spot, won't it?"

Phil looked up suddenly. "Why should it?"

Bimbo poked at the bottom of his glass with the straw, "Isn't the city engineer supposed to see that buildings are built so they won't fall down?" he said.

"It was an accident. An accident can happen any time."

"Sure, I know," Bimbo said. Then he went on stubbornly. "But isn't it his job to inspect those buildings to see that accidents don't happen?"

Phil frowned at Bimbo. "Look, stupid," he said, "the city engineer doesn't inspect the buildings himself. He has building inspectors to do that. Besides, Dad's been city engineer here for twelve years, and nothing like this ever happened before. Take it easy. Dad will have some kind of an investigation, and then we'll know for sure what happened."

"OK," Bimbo said. He looked at Phil's glass as Phil slid out from under the table. "You didn't touch your root beer."

"I didn't want it."

Bimbo looked at the drink longingly. "Maybe if Gracie put a scoop of ice cream in it, I'd . . ."

"I'm a working man," Phil snapped. "I can't sit around and watch you stuff yourself. I have to get back to work. Besides, I have to stop by Bud's garage and have him check my water pump." He turned and started for the front door.

Bimbo gave the drink one last look, then followed Phil.

Prater's Garage was a hangout for a group of the older citizens of Seacrest, and Bud Prater made it comfortable for them by providing a row of chairs along the front. The usual bunch was there when Phil and Bimbo drove up. Cap Winters was there as always, hunched over in his chair, his cane held between his knees. Cap was a second cousin of Phil's father and often came to their house for Sunday dinner and to spin sea yarns for Phil.

Bimbo walked over to talk to the group, and Phil went into the garage to find Bud Prater. After Bud had promised to check the water pump, Phil started back to join Bimbo and the others. He was passing the cold drink machine when he heard his friend's voice.

"It was an accident. An accident can happen any time," Bimbo was saying.

The words were the same Phil had used back at the malt shop. The group was talking about the wall collapsing, but it was too late for Phil to turn back now. He walked on and stood beside Bimbo. "Hello, Cap," he said. "Have you been giving them some of your old sea stories?"

Cap's head bobbed defiantly. "Victor Sanchez is dead," he said coldly.

The news staggered Phil, but the old man's attitude baffled him. "I'm sorry," he said, shaking his head. "Gosh, I'm awfully sorry."

The old man's frosty eyes stayed on Phil. "Sorry won't bring Victor back," he said.

Phil was bewildered. Cap's tone had been almost an accusation, as though somehow Phil had been responsible for the man's death. He looked at the others. They sat in a line, like a jury, and their eyes were as cold and as hostile as Cap's. Phil felt a small sense of panic building up inside him. It was as though he had been set down in the midst of some horrible nightmare. He wanted to protest, but he hadn't done anything.

The man on the end turned back to Bimbo. "An accident like that don't just happen, son. There's got to be a reason for it."

"Somebody was to blame," said another.

Phil looked at Bimbo, but Bimbo was staring at the ground.

"I've been expecting something like this to happen," the man on the end said. "Our taxes go up and up, but we get less and less to show for them."

The burly man who worked as a brake specialist for Bud stood at the corner of the building, a soft drink in his hand. "It's that bunch down at city hall," he said. "They're all as crooked as a dog's hind leg."

The brake man had come to Seacrest less than a year before, and Phil had never liked him—or his son Lonnie, either. Lonnie was about Phil's age and hung around the garage a lot. The boy was sullen, like his father, and Phil had never made any effort to get acquainted. Now the man's words stung Phil into replying. "Not everyone down there at city hall is a crook," he said sharply.

"Phil's father is the city engineer," the man on the end explained.

The brake man swallowed the rest of his drink, dropped the empty bottle into the rack, and wiped his mouth on the back of his hand. He squinted at Phil. "So your old man's the only honest one down there," he said. "He's the one straight snake in a nest of crooked ones, is that right?" He looked over at the others and winked. "The way I hear it, you can throw up any kind of a claptrap building in this town, as long as you pay the inspectors to look the other way."

Rage swelled up in Phil and choked him. He clenched his fists and glared at the man. "That's a lie," he managed to say. "That's a dirty lie, and you know it."

"We know this guy Sanchez was killed when one of those buildings fell down," the man said, drawing his lip back. "Somebody got paid off, and somebody got killed because of it. In my book that's murder."

Phil couldn't bring himself to look around at the others; he knew what he would see. They were agreeing with the brake man, not with him. Suddenly his frustrated anger built up and came to a head in a blaze of uncontrollable rage. Unfortunately, Lonnie chose that moment to walk around the corner and stop beside his father. "What's the beef?" he asked, looking at Phil.

The son looked enough like the father to be a substitute. With a yell, Phil leaped forward and hit the boy in the face with all his strength. There was no science in the overhand punch, but it caught Lonnie unprepared and he staggered backward, his arms flailing.

Phil felt the heavy weight of the brake specialist hit him with a body block, and before he could recover, his arms were pinned behind him.

"Take it easy," Bimbo said into his ear.

Lonnie had his hand over his nose. Then he raised his fists and advanced menacingly.

Phil was bracing himself to pull away, when Bud Prater pushed his way between the combatants. "All right, break it up," he ordered curtly. "I won't have any fighting around here."

"He started it," Lonnie said.

"I saw it," Bud said, his voice cold. He turned to Phil. "I fixed your water pump. I think you'd better get out of here." When Phil reached back to take out his wallet, Bud shook him off. "You don't owe me anything." He turned and walked into the garage.

As he and Bimbo walked to the car, Phil knew every eye on his back was hostile. He climbed into the car and slammed the door. "Stupid jerks," he said viciously as he put the car into gear.

Phil sat slumped in a chair against the wall, staring down at the strip of adhesive tape across his knuckles. Bimbo walked around the office, while Scotty sat behind his desk. Bimbo had tried to make a joke of the incident at the garage. He had staggered backward, throwing his arms around, do- ing an imitation of Lonnie, but Scotty hadn't smiled.

Phil had not tried to explain. He was still too confused to

know why he had acted that way. He certainly couldn't explain it so it made any sense. There wasn't any sense to anything that had happened at the garage. Some fellows who had always been old friends had suddenly turned against him, and he had lashed out.

Scotty filled his pipe, and after it was lighted he swung his swivel chair around. "Phil, you must realize the amount of tension there is in town against city hall."

"I guess so," Phil muttered, keeping his eyes down. He had known that Mayor Tom Warford was considered a crooked politician, but then he thought that most politicians were considered crooked. The fact that his father worked for city hall had never made him connect the city engineer's job with a crooked administration. Phil had a general idea of what his father did, and it was a pretty dull, routine job. It was nothing to be proud about, but certainly nothing to be ashamed of.

"Your father holds a pretty important job here in town," Scotty said quietly.

Phil had never thought of his father as being important. He had never thought about him much as an individual, except to know that he was a stoic, quiet man who kept his thoughts to himself. His father was a good man, Phil was sure of that, and nobody was going to convince him otherwise. "I guess he does," he said in a low voice.

"Seacrest has changed a great deal in the past few years," Scotty went on. "You're eighteen now, so you probably don't remember when it was just a quiet little village near the coast. The truck farmers used to haul their own produce down to Los Angeles. There were lots of poultry farms, but little or no industry here in town."

Bimbo walked over and dropped into a chair. "Sounds like life was a drag around here then," he said.

Scotty smiled slightly. "There are plenty of citizens who wish it was that way again. Life wasn't very complicated—no graft, no gambling, no crime waves."

"You sound like my father," Bimbo said.

"Your father is one of the conservative element, yes."

Bimbo nodded. "If conservative means square, man, that's my father. He still thinks a space suit is something you buy to grow in."

Phil only half heard the conversation that was going on. He was still trying to reconcile the faint image that he had of his father with someone whom the whole town could get aroused about. He shifted his weight, but remained silent.

Scotty puffed thoughtfully on his pipe before he continued. "Then about ten years ago they built a missile test site near here. After that came the bases and the tracking stations. The electronics plants spread out from Los Angeles, and the next thing we knew, Seacrest was a thriving little city."

"Sounds like a good deal to me," Phil said.

"That's what the merchants thought at first. People flocked in, they bought new homes in the housing tracts, groceries, and clothing. But then the fast-buck boys moved in, too, and before we woke up, they had a stranglehold on the city government. Tom Warford got in as mayor. He put Benny Shad in as police chief, and from then on Seacrest was a wide open town. Gambling joints sprung up on Ramona Road like weeds."

"I thought Ramona Road was always like that," Bimbo said.

Scotty smiled wryly. "It used to run through bean fields."

As Scotty talked, Phil began to realize that he knew as little about his own home town as he did about his father. He had always taken it for granted that his father was what he was and that the town had always been like this. Now he straightened up in his chair. "If the citizens here are so sore at Mayor Warford, why don't they vote him out? They still have elections, don't they?"

Scotty put his pipe down and clasped his hands on the desk. "Some of the citizens tried to do something," he said. "Bimbo's father and Virgil Charters formed what they called the Citizens' Protective League, but there's been so much internal dissention that they've never done much."

"You should hear my father spout about that league at home," Bimbo said.

"Your father has a big investment in his department store, Bimbo. He's vitally interested in the future of Seacrest."

"Virgil Charters owns a lot of real estate, doesn't he?" Phil said.

Scotty nodded. "Unless a town is built on sound government, property values can go down. At one time, Charters owned one of the biggest feed and grain mills in this part of the country. He still has his office down there in the old building, but he closed the mill years ago, when the poultry farms disappeared."

Phil massaged his sore knuckles. "I ask you again, if the

people of this town are so sore about things, why don't they vote Mayor Warford out?"

"It isn't that simple," Scotty said. "Once a crooked political machine gets into power, it's hard to get them out. They have their own police department to back them up, and there are always voters who are looking for favors. Some people think Warford isn't the real boss at all, that there's somebody here in town who is the power behind the throne. If Tom Warford is only a figurehead, the Citizens' League will have to root out the real boss before they can ever clean up Seacrest."

Phil remembered the anger and hostility of the old men at the garage. He was filled with resentment now that he had heard Scotty's story. Why weren't the men fighting Tom Warford instead of his father? They were the ones who had let the crooked machine get into power, not Phil Martinson; he wasn't even allowed to vote yet. It seemed to him that they were looking for a goat to blame, to cover up their own mistakes. "Do you have any idea who the real boss is?" When Scotty shook his head, Phil asked, "Is my father a member of the Citizens' Protective League?"

Scotty rubbed his jaw. He studied the top of his desk. "No, he isn't, Phil. I'm afraid he's considered to be on the other side of the fence." Scotty looked over. "You see, as long as your father is city engineer, he's part of the city government, and I'm afraid most people lump them all together as a bunch of crooks."

Phil's resentment grew at the injustice of this. His resentment turned to anger, and he had the same compulsion to lash out. This time he kept his anger under control. He swallowed hard and looked up. "Did you say Tom Warford has been mayor here less than ten years?" he said, careful to keep his voice level.

"That's right."

"But my father has been city engineer for over twelve years. He had that job before Warford ever got into power."

"That's right. And before he took that job, your father had a small building business."

"If they thought he was all right then, why would they think he was crooked now?"

Scotty toyed with the pipe on his desk. He studied it as he spoke. "The people here have a right to blame everyone down at city hall," he said slowly. "They've seen some honest men sell out in the past." He looked over at Phil. "They convict your father just because he's still at city hall," he said. "Warford has managed to get rid of anyone who refused to play ball."

"So they think Dad has sold out and is working for Mayor Warford. I get the picture. Most of the good citizens here think I'm the son of a crook. What do I do now, slink down alleys and hide in doorways?"

Scotty got up and came around from behind his desk. "This has been a tough blow for you, Phil. I thought you understood how things were, but there's no sense in trying to dramatize the situation. You can't slink around with your tail between your legs. You're going to have to face up to facts."

"Like how?" Phil said, staring at the floor.

"Well, certainly not the way you did over at Bud's garage today. That was kid stuff, the way you used to settle things on the playground when you thought somebody was picking on you. You're eighteen now, Phil, and you're going to have to act like a mature person, not a kid. If you intend to try to change a person's opinion of your father, you won't do it by poking him in the nose." Scotty walked back and sat down. "I'm sorry, Phil," he said gruffly, "but I didn't think this was any time to pull punches."

Heavy silence hung in the office until a chair scraped and Bimbo got up. He walked over and stood before Phil. "My father is a big shot in this Citizens' League," he said soberly. "Tonight when he gets home, I'll beard the lion in his den. I'll talk to him and see if I can't make him see the light."

"I've known your father a good many years," Scotty said drily. "And, Bimbo, I'd say your chances of convincing Samuel Barnes that he is wrong are about the same as your chances of crawling through that keyhole."

Bimbo solemnly looked at the tiny opening in the door. "I can try," he said.

Phil looked up and gave him a twisted grin. "Thanks, pal," he said. "It means a lot to know you're willing to try."

CHAPTER 3

PHIL MARTINSON had lived in the same house all his life. It was a somber, two-story place in the older section of town, built by Carl Martinson shortly after his marriage to Phil's mother.

Two years after Phil's birth, his mother had died of pneumonia, and Mrs. Flemming, a childless widow, had been brought in to care for baby Phil. At the time, the arrangement was to be only temporary, but the lady had proved so efficient and had taken things over so completely that she had stayed on ever since.

Phil never thought of Mrs. Flemming as a mother. He had never known his real mother, but he had accepted the cheerful little widow as a part of his life. Phil was very fond of Mrs. Flemming.

The housekeeper was a creature of habit, who wouldn't have allowed an earthquake to upset the household routine. At six, on the evening of the building accident, dinner was on the table, although Carl Martinson had not yet come home. "Maybe we'd better wait for Dad," Phil suggested.

"Food was made to be eaten while it's hot," Mrs. Flemming said, pushing him toward the table. "A person's body is

accustomed to food at a certain time. Change it and you upset your innards."

Phil sat down and waited, while Mrs. Flemming clasped
her hands before her, bowed her head, and said grace. When
she was through, her head bobbed up. "I'm keeping your
father's dinner in the oven," she said by way of explanation.

"I'm afraid I'm not very hungry," Phil said quickly to ward
off her fussing at him for not eating.

"Fiddlesticks," Mrs. Flemming said, passing the meat, "a
growing boy is always hungry."

Phil took small portions and ate slowly. He really wasn't
hungry—he was too concerned with his problem. He tuned
out Mrs. Flemming's cheerful chatter while he concentrated
on what he intended to do that evening. He was going to
have a serious talk with his father.

Although Phil and his father were alone in the world, this
didn't seem to have brought them close together. There
had never been a serious clash between them, and there was
no hostility, yet they had never had a close father and son
relationship. Always there had been a cool wall of reserve
separating them. Phil had often wanted to know his father
better, but Carl Martinson was a man of few words, who
seemed to find it difficult, if not impossible, to show his emo-
tions.

Phil knew he was faced with a difficult problem in trying
to get his father to confide in him. He had tried in the past
and had always failed. Each time he had wanted to have a
heart-to-heart talk, the session had ended with each of them
staring at the floor in embarrassed silence. This time it had
to be different.

Phil finished his dinner, asked to be excused, and went into the living room to watch television. Twenty minutes later his father came in, picked up the evening paper, and sank down into the easy chair under the floor lamp. He was a man of stocky build, with heavy hands. His hair was thinning on the top, and Phil noted with a start that his father's face looked hollow and gaunt.

Phil snapped off the television set and crossed the room to stand beside his father's chair. "You were late tonight, Dad."

His father looked up. "It was business." There was weariness in his voice.

"I called your office around five, but you were out."

Mr. Martinson sighed. "I wasn't in the office much today," he said and looked down at his paper.

Phil took a deep breath. "I was out at that building on Ramona Road this morning, Dad." He paused a moment. "I guess you know that Victor Sanchez died." He thought he saw the newspaper tremble.

"Yes, I heard. It was a terrible thing."

"Victor was a good friend of ours."

"Victor was a fine man," his father said in a tight voice and started to unfold his newspaper.

Phil felt a surge of panic. This was a signal their talk was over. The wall had risen between them again, but this time Phil was determined to tear it down. Impulsively, he reached over and grabbed the newspaper from his father's hands. "Dad," he said quickly, "listen . . ." He plunged on before his father could speak. "Do you remember a couple of years ago, when I first started to drive? Do you remember how I sneaked your car out one day when you weren't here and bashed the fender in?"

His father's eyes were patient. "Has something happened, son?"

Phil shook his head impatiently. "No, I'm trying to explain something else. Do you remember at first I told you I didn't know how it happened. Then later I confessed I'd sneaked the car out and hit a tree?"

"I remember."

"Remember what you told me then? You told me we should always be frank and honest with each other."

Carl Martinson glanced up, a puzzled look in his eyes. "Are you in some kind of trouble, son? Are you trying to tell me . . . ?"

"It's not me that's in trouble," Phil said harshly, then he stopped. "Look, Dad," he said quietly, "I know why you were late tonight, and I know why you weren't in your office today." He looked down on his father's bowed head. "Dad, what made that wall collapse and kill Victor?"

Mr. Martinson shook his head slowly without looking up. "We don't know yet," he said in a low voice. He put out his hand. "Now if I could have my paper, please."

Phil pulled the newspaper back. "I don't mean to be insolent," he said desperately, "but you did say we should be frank and honest with each other—that rule should work both ways, shouldn't it?"

His father stared at his big hands a long time before he spoke. "I suppose it should," he said.

"I'm not asking out of idle curiosity. I think I have a right to know. Look, today I pulled a dumb kid stunt over at Bud

Prater's garage. It was my fault, but maybe part of the reason I acted so stupidly was because I didn't understand. You'd never told me how things were. I didn't even know what was going on around town."

Carl Martinson pushed himself halfway out of the chair. "What happened?" he demanded.

"Nothing much. What happened today wasn't anything. It's what *is* happening every day here in Seacrest that's important. Dad, can't we talk this thing out? I'm eighteen years old now; I'm not a kid any more."

Slowly his father lowered himself back down into the chair. He was silent as he kneaded the flesh at the bridge of his nose. "Tell me, what did happen today, son?" he finally said.

Phil told him how Cap and the rest had practically accused Carl Martinson of being responsible for Victor Sanchez's death. He told him how the brake man had said the city engineer's office accepted bribes. But he glossed over the part where he'd hit Lonnie. "You see, Dad," he finished up, "I'm in this thing, too, now."

Phil thought his father looked smaller, squashed down in the chair that way. He could see the light gleam on his bare scalp through the strands of hair. Phil had never thought of his father as being of any special age, but now it was a shock to see him looking so old and worn.

Mr. Martinson uttered a deep sigh. "I suppose it was stupid of me to think I could keep this mess from touching you," he said sadly.

Phil pulled a straight chair over and sat facing his father. "Forget me, Dad. Nobody's blaming me for anything. It's you I'm worried about. Now I'd like to know everything that has happened so far."

"It's hard for a man to admit he's a failure, especially to his own son. I'm a good man working with my hands, but I'm no good at a desk job. I should have stayed in the building business."

"Dad, I don't understand why you took this city engineer job in the first place."

"You might say I was pressured into it," his father said. "Samuel Barnes, Virgil Charters, and some of the others thought the town needed someone in there who knew the building game."

"But they're the fellows who are knifing you in the back now."

"They're critical, all right," his father admitted. "But things have changed since I took that job. Then, it was all pretty simple. I had to make sure the streets and sewers were laid right and that all buildings conformed to our building code. If I do say so myself, I did a good job, an honest job. I only wish things were the same now."

"Scotty said about the same thing."

"We thought our little town growing up into a city was a fine thing," his father went on. "In some ways it was good, but then other things developed that weren't so desirable."

"Like Mayor Tom Warford," Phil said.

"Like Tom Warford. When I first realized that things weren't right down there at city hall, I tried to go on about my business and ignore them. But then they began to involve themselves in my office, and before long I found myself mixed up in this dirty mess. I had to fight every move they made. They weren't interested in the future of Seacrest, but only in the money they could make."

"It must have been tough, fighting alone," Phil said.

"The worst part was that I knew I was no match for that crowd. I'm only a small-town contractor—I don't know any of their crooked tricks. I made mistakes because I wasn't smart enough to see what that crowd was up to."

"But you did fight them."

"Yes," his father said slowly, "if you consider trying to give Seacrest an honest building program fighting, I fought them."

Phil thought of how long the mayor had been in office and realized that his father had been fighting his own private war all that time. Phil wondered how a man could endure what his father had gone through without ever a word of complaint. Even now he wasn't blaming the citizens who had turned against him. "Why don't you go to Mr. Barnes, Mr. Charters, and the rest? Tell them what you're doing."

His father looked mildly surprised. "Why should I tell them that I'm trying to do the job I was hired to do?" he asked.

"But they're making you the goat."

"No, son, the citizens of Seacrest aren't making me the goat. Mayor Warford is making me the goat."

Phil reached over and placed his hand on his father's knee. "Look, Dad, the people here in town think you're crooked because you're staying down there at city hall. Why don't you quit that job? That would prove that you weren't in with Warford."

Carl Martinson shook his head firmly. "I can't," he said.

"I'm about the last honest man in office. If I quit, that would mean complete surrender to Warford and his crowd. I may not be able to do much, but I'm still a brake to keep them from going hog wild. I was born in this town, son, and I feel a strong responsibility as a citizen of Seacrest."

"Some of the rest of them who were born here don't appreciate your efforts."

"I'm not looking for appreciation. I think I know what's right, and I have to keep on doing that as long as I can."

Phil realized that it was useless to try to change his father's mind. "Has Warford ever tried to get rid of you?" he asked.

"Up until now I've provided an air of respectability for his administration. But he would dump me in a minute if he saw the chance."

Phil rose and walked around the room. As he looked at his father, he now saw an altogether different man from the one who had sat there before. It was as though Phil had met his father for the first time in his life. Until now he had regarded his father as someone who had paid for the food and clothing, who had provided the roof over their heads, and who had given him his education. Phil remembered with a twinge that at times he had even been ashamed of his father for his rather slow, clumsy manner. "Dad," he said, "what really caused that wall to collapse today?"

Mr. Martinson mulled this question over before he answered. "I made an unofficial inspection," he said slowly. "I think it was faulty concrete." He looked up. "You see, the specifications on that job called for a special mix. It was to be delivered, ready-mixed, and had to be signed for on the job. The concrete in that wall wasn't the mix specified."

Phil walked back to face his father. "You said the mix had to be signed for. Who signed that certificate?"

"One of the inspectors."

Phil felt a twinge of excitement. "That's a starting point," he said. "If the man signed for the wrong mix, then that lets you off the hook."

"The inspector is one of Warford's men," his father said flatly.

"I don't care if he is. What we have to do is prove he signed for the wrong mix. If he did it on purpose, then that could be murder."

Carl Martinson looked up. "Murder is a hard word," he said.

"That's what they're accusing you of around town." Phil began to pace the room. "You get hold of that certificate the first thing tomorrow," he said. "You hold on to it. That's going to be our trump card."

Carl Martison shook his head slowly. "You don't know Warford and his crowd, son. I know them—I've fought them almost ten years. The contractor who's building that job is from Los Angeles and he has connections. Warford will move fast to cover up."

Phil slammed his fist into his palm. "OK then, we'll move faster. This time we're not going to let Warford get the jump on you; we'll jump first."

His father rose to his feet slowly. "Don't get mixed up in this, son. It's a dirty, rotten business and no place for a boy."

He clutched Phil's arm. "You'll be going off to school in the fall. Don't do anything that could hurt you in college."

His father's words brought Phil up short. In his burst of excitement, he had completely forgotten his own plans. Now all that seemed trivial compared with what his father faced. "I'm not going away until this has been cleared up."

His father frowned. "Your education is important, son. You've planned a long time to . . ."

"I'm staying," Phil said firmly. "You might never have noticed it, but I've got some of Carl Martinson's stubbornness, too."

CHAPTER 4

THE NEXT MORNING, Phil carried his problem to work, but he did not mention his talk of the evening before to Scotty. Phil felt that while Scotty had been sympathetic, still, he seemed to have a reserved opinion of Carl Martinson. Now Phil could understand that attitude, and he had no intention of trying to drag anyone else into the fight.

There was always plenty to do around the studio, so while Phil cleaned the darkroom and mixed chemicals, he planned his strategy. His plan was to attack Mayor Warford first. His father's method of doing a good job in silence hadn't worked. This would take a new approach—a hard-driving, aggressive attack on the administration. His father had borne the brunt alone for so long that he was now capable of doing little—Phil knew he would have to do most of the fighting for the Martinson family from here on in.

At eleven o'clock Scotty called him outside. "I don't have anything lined up today," he said. "I think I'll drive down to Los Angeles and pick up some supplies. You tend to the store this afternoon."

Phil was glad to be alone; it gave him a chance to think without interruption. He had decided that the certificate, signed by someone even though the concrete mix was faulty, was their strongest weapon. He realized how close to the breaking point his father must be, to have overlooked that evidence.

Three times Phil called the city hall to see if his father had the certificate, but each time he was told Carl Martinson was out. He was probably on Ramona Road, but Phil was tied up at the studio and couldn't go there to check.

He sat at Scotty's desk and drew a line down the center of a piece of paper. On one side he listed the charges that could be made against Mayor Warford. On the other side he wrote the charges against his father. He frowned when he saw they were about equal in length. Phil looked up as the front door burst open and Bimbo lumbered in. Phil shoved the paper under the desk blotter. "Hi," he said.

Bimbo looked at the blotter. "What are you hiding?" he asked suspiciously. "A love letter or something?"

"No, it's not a love letter. It's something personal."

"A love letter's personal, isn't it? I don't know anything more personal . . ."

"Oh, knock it off, will you? What do you want?"

Bimbo stopped to scratch his head. "I dunno, I must have been on my way to the malt shop."

"I can't go. Scotty's gone for the day." Phil looked at his watch. "Wow, it's three o'clock and I didn't have any lunch. How about bringing me back a hamburger and a shake?"

Bimbo brought back food for both of them, and the boys ate in silence until Bimbo suddenly spoke. "I talked to my father last night," he said with his mouth full.

The statement snapped Phil's thoughts back. "Oh," he said, frowning, "what did you talk about?"

Bimbo looked hurt. "Why, about your father," he said. "I told you yesterday I'd talk to him about . . ."

"Sure, I remember," Phil said soothingly, "I was thinking about something else. What did he say?"

"You don't expect me to give you the whole lecture, word for word, do you?" Bimbo chewed for a moment, then went on. "The gist of it was that I have certain responsibilities as a citizen and that every citizen should have a keen interest in maintaining a clean civic government. Then he told me I wasn't dry behind the ears yet and to stop poking my nose into something I didn't know anything about."

Phil thought of his talk with his own father. "That's too bad," he said.

"He didn't actually call your father a crook, though."

"That was nice of him," Phil said sarcastically.

Bimbo finished the last of his milk shake, and as he put the carton down, his mouth dropped open.

"All right," Phil said, "what did you think of?"

"Nothing."

"Don't tell me that. Every time you have a thought, your face shows it as if you'd punched the button on a cash register."

Bimbo closed his mouth. "Well, I just remembered that I was at the drug store reading magazines before I came here. Some fellow was there, talking loud about your father."

"Who was he?"

"I don't know him," Bimbo said, "but I think I've seen him down at city hall. Hey, Phil, what's a variance?"

"It's permission for a change in the building code. What did this fellow say about a variance?"

"He said the engineer's office had allowed a variance out there on that job, and that was what had caused the accident."

Mayor Warford has fired the opening gun against Dad, Phil thought. While he had been sitting around here, writing things on paper, Warford had gone into action. His father hadn't mentioned any variance last night, but then his father had been pretty upset. Perhaps it had escaped his mind. Phil made a mental note to ask him about any variance he had allowed. Phil was so deep in his own thoughts that he spoke without realizing it. "I've got to do something, but fast," he said.

"Like what?" Bimbo said. "What are we going to do?"

Phil looked up. "*We're* not going to do anything, sonny. This is a private affair."

Bimbo got up. "Now wait just a doggone minute," he said angrily. "I'm your old pal Bimbo, remember?"

Phil managed a grin. "Sure, I remember," he said. "But you can't help me out. Your father is on the other side."

"What's my father got to do with it?"

Phil shook his head. "It's got everything to do with it, Bimbo. I appreciate all you've done, but you can't come out in an open fight against your own father."

"He's usually against me."

"But that's different, Bimbo."

Bimbo came over and leaned across the desk. "Look," he said, "my father has already taken my car away from me for something or other he didn't like. My allowance is overdrawn for six weeks ahead. I'm bound to get lectures, no matter what I do, so what have I got to lose by throwing in with you?" Bimbo waited a moment, then blurted out. "Besides, I want to prove to this town they're lucky to have a man like your father as city engineer."

Phil stood and put out his hand. "That last statement sold me, son. From now on we're in this thing together."

Phil spent the next few minutes bringing Bimbo up to date on what he had learned from his father the evening before. He explained the importance of the certificate that had been signed for the substitute mix. In talking it over, the boys decided that important as the certificate was, they would need more evidence. They puzzled over Mayor Warford's use of the variance as a weapon against Phil's father, then decided to wait until they had talked to Carl Martinson about that.

They thought city hall itself might be a source of information, but both boys knew there was little chance that they could find out anything. Then Phil thought of Jon Hansen, whom he knew slightly through his father. Jon Hansen was the clean-up custodian at the city hall. He worked nights, and the boys agreed that anyone who could poke around in wastepaper baskets could well have access to important information.

Before Phil closed up the studio for the day, he and Bimbo agreed to meet that evening and go to city hall. They formed no clear-cut plan of operation, but decided to play it by ear once they were there.

Mr. Martinson was not home for dinner that evening, so Phil had no chance to ask him about the variance. Phil ate, then left the house without telling Mrs. Flemming where he was going.

The Seacrest city hall was housed in a buff stucco building of Spanish architecture and stood behind a carefully trimmed lawn. There were a few lighted windows as the boys walked up to the entrance, but no one was in the rotunda.

They had walked halfway down one of the corridors, when a khaki cap, over a long face, popped out of a doorway. "What are you boys doing in here?" the old man demanded.

"Good evening, Mr. Hansen," Phil said, stepping forward.

Jon Hansen thrust his head out to peer. "Well, it's the Martinson boy," he said. "I'm afraid your father ain't in his office. He don't come around here at nights much anymore."

"I know." Phil swung his hand up. "Don't let us keep you from your work, Mr. Hansen."

"Thank ye, I won't. You can come in here if you want to talk. I'm waxing furniture right now," he said, walking over to the single desk in the office. "Seems like it always needs waxing."

"I guess so." Phil looked around the office. "Who works in here?" he asked.

"This is Mr. Leppert's office. He's private secretary or something to Mayor Warford." The old man carried a cloth through the door behind the desk, into a small lavatory. "Mr. Leppert's a pretty important man, I guess," he said, as he dampened the cloth under the faucet. "He's right on top of everything that happens around here."

"I'll bet you know a lot that goes on around here, too."

The old custodian laid the cloth down and came around the desk. "I know enough to keep my mouth shut," he said. "Son, I know what's happening to your father. I've known

Carl Martinson for a long time. I like Carl a lot, and I'd like to help him, but a body can't call his soul his own around here anymore. I've worked hard, and I'm due to retire on a pension next year. But if somebody gets the idea I'm in the way, they'd fire me tomorrow. I can't do it, son. I'm looking forward to that pension to live on."

"I see," Phil said quietly. He watched the old man pick up his wax and cloths.

Jon Hansen walked toward the door. "Even the walls got ears around here," he grumbled. "Somebody spying on you from behind every door."

"He sounded like he was scared," Bimbo said when Hansen had trudged down the corridor.

"He was scared," Phil said. "I guess we can't look for much help there." He glanced around. "You go on out and close the door. This is as good a place as any for me to start. You go on down the hall and see what you can find."

"What am I looking for?"

Phil gave Bimbo a shove. "Who knows? But get going."

Bimbo started for the door. "I don't know," he said, his voice wavering. "Since I heard Hansen, I don't think I want to get caught snooping around."

"Don't get caught then. And snap off that light on your way out."

Even with the lights off, the office was filled with a soft glow from the frosted panel in the door. Phil moved over to the desk and pulled the top drawer open. There was nothing in there but an assortment of pencils and paper clips. He opened the deep side drawer and groaned at the sight of the mass of paper-filled folders. There must be a thousand different pieces of paper there, he thought. It would take a week to go through each one.

Phil started to close the drawer, then stopped. The job looked hopeless, but if anybody had important papers, it would be Warford's private secretary. The mayor himself wouldn't keep evidence in his own office. More than likely, what Phil was looking for was somewhere in that drawer.

He knew he would need light to read by, and he'd reached over to snap on the desk lamp when a sound in the corridor stopped his hand in mid-air. It was the sharp click of leather heels on the floor, approaching the door.

Phil closed the drawer and looked around. It was too late to slip out the door, so he crossed behind the desk and went into the lavatory. He pulled the door almost closed and waited.

The footsteps stopped. The door opened and a dark shape entered. After closing the door again, the figure moved quickly across and snapped on the desk lamp. In the instant before he pulled back, Phil saw a small, dark man who moved with quick, nervous motions.

Phil huddled back against the wall in the darkness. He heard keys being jangled, then the sound of a cabinet door being opened. He took a quiet step forward and peeked through the crack. The man was less than six feet away, with his back turned as he worked over something on the desk. The man payed out an electric cord, and carried it over to the wall socket. Phil saw that a portable tape recorder had been set up on the desk.

Before the man returned, Phil pulled back against the wall again. Out in the office there was a series of clicks as the telephone was dialed, then a pause. "This is Leppert. Is everything ready?" the man in the office said. There was silence, broken by the whirring of the motor of the tape recorder. Suddenly there was a scrambled, high-pitched babble of gibberish that lasted only seconds, then stopped abruptly.

"Did you get it?" the man asked. "OK, same time tomorrow night." Phil heard the telephone being replaced.

At first Phil had been unable to tell what the sound had been; then he realized it was a tape being played faster than the speed at which it had been recorded. He moved up to the door again and saw the man take the reel from the machine, put the reel into a box, and drop the box into his coat pocket. The man looked down at his hands and took a step toward the lavatory. He glanced at his watch, then hurriedly put the lid back on the tape recorder and placed it in the cabinet. Phil had remained frozen while the man worked, and he didn't relax until the door was again closed and he heard the leather heels clicking back down the hall.

Phil stepped out of the lavatory. The office was just as it had been before the man came in, and Phil knew the tape recorder in the cabinet would do him no good, even if he could get it out. The man had taken the reel with him. But this new development had caused him to give up the idea of going through the papers in the desk.

Phil opened the door and peered out before he stepped into the hallway and closed Leppert's office door behind him. He could hear the sound of a pail being banged on the floor in the direction of the front entrance, so he walked quietly the other way. He whistled softly as he passed each open office door, until he heard an answering whistle and Bimbo came out. "Let's get out of here," Phil whispered.

"I didn't find anything," Bimbo whispered back.

"I did."

"What did you find?"

"C'mon, let's get out of here before Mr. Hansen comes looking for us and throws us out."

Jon Hansen supervised a crew of cleaning women, and when the boys passed through the rotunda on their way to the front door, Phil saw the old custodian talking to one of the women. Hansen did not look up or act as though he knew they were there.

Bimbo pestered Phil for information as soon as they were outside the building, but Phil waited until they were in the car before he answered. "I didn't find anything I can show you, Bimbo," he said. "I heard something, but I don't know what I heard."

"You're giving me the runaround," Bimbo said peevishly.

"I'm not." Phil started the car and drove away. "I'm trying to figure it out in my own mind." He drove in silence until they reached a corner near Bimbo's home. "I'd better let you out here," he said. "If your father sees you get out of my car, you'll be in for another lecture."

Bimbo climbed out without speaking.

"Scotty has an appointment tomorrow afternoon," Phil said. "Drop around to the studio. I think I'll have this thing worked out by then, and I'll be able to explain everything."

"All right," Bimbo said grudgingly, "I'll be there."

On his way to work the next morning, Phil stopped in at Bill Hootner's camera shop. When he entered the studio, he found the desk piled high with supplies Scotty had brought back from Los Angeles. He spent the next hour unpacking the film and chemicals and storing them away. When he had finished, Scotty handed him a packet of negatives he had pulled from the file cabinet in the office.

Phil made contact prints by placing the sensitized paper over each negative and then exposing them to a light in the contact printer. After they had been souped and dried, he took the negative-size contact prints in and laid them on the desk.

Scotty studied each one before he flipped it over and wrote how he wanted the enlargements cropped and how many of the large prints he wanted Phil to make.

Phil spent the rest of the morning at the enlarger and with the developer pans. He enjoyed this work and was so familiar with the procedure that his motions were almost automatic. The photographic safe lights could be used when making prints, and their faint glow left the room in semi-darkness. The quiet solitude helped Phil to concentrate on what he had heard in Leppert's office the evening before. He was so deeply engrossed in his problem that he jumped when Scotty entered the room.

Scotty wanted Phil to go to lunch, so Scotty could leave for his appointment as soon as Phil got back.

That afternoon, Phil was alone in the studio, sorting out the glossy prints he had made, when Bimbo came in.

"Are you ready to tell me now what you heard?" Bimbo asked grumpily.

"Sure." Phil put the prints into a manila envelope and dropped them into a drawer. "I'm sorry I couldn't explain last night," he said. "But the whole thing was jumbled up in my brain, and I couldn't tell you until I had the answer figured out myself."

"What's the answer?"

Phil went to the closet and brought back a small, flat plastic box. He placed this on the desk. "Bill Hootner sells tape recorders in his camera shop," he said. "I've always traded with him, so this morning I stopped by and borrowed this machine. It's a compact transistor model that runs on batteries; you don't need to plug it into the house circuit."

"What are you trying to do, sell it to me?"

Phil ignored Bimbo's remark and took the lid off the box. "Now I want to show you something," he said, threading the tape through the sound-head slot and securing the end to the empty reel on the other side. He plugged in the small microphone cord and flipped the switch that set the machine in motion. "Bimbo Barnes, you are a knucklehead. Do you understand that?" he said into the mike.

After Phil had run the tape back, he made an adjustment and started it forward again. "Bimbo Barnes, you are a knucklehead. Do you understand that?" the machine said.

"Sure, I understand it," Bimbo said. "I mean I understood what you said."

"Then listen to this." Phil made another adjustment and repeated the procedure. This time there was only a short burst of high-pitched gibberish from the machine.

"Nobody could understand that," Bimbo said.

"Exactly," Phil said, snapping off the switch. "Almost all

tape recorders are made to run at two speeds. The slow speed passes the tape by the sound heads at three and three quarters inches per second. Then there is a high speed that runs it through twice as fast, or seven and one half inches per second. Do you get that?"

"Sure, if you record speech at the slow speed and then run it through twice as fast, you can't understand it."

"Right. Now that kind of gibberish is what I heard Leppert play last night. There was a message recorded at the slow speed on the tape he had, and he'd turned the machine up on high speed to play it back."

"So what have you got if nobody could understand it?"

"That's what I thought at first," Phil said. "But what you don't know is that Leppert played that gibberish into the telephone. Now suppose somebody on the other end of the line had another tape recorder running at high speed, recording this gibberish." Phil waited for his statement to sink in. When Bimbo nodded that he understood, Phil went on. "Now suppose the fellow at the other end took this gibberish and played it back at the speed at which it had been originally recorded?"

Bimbo stared, owl-eyed. "He'd have a decoding machine."

Phil nodded. "You're so right. The thing is almost foolproof. They can send any kind of a message and nobody can pick it up unless he's waiting with a tape recorder running at high speed. I was right there and heard the whole thing, but I didn't understand one single word."

"Real slick," Bimbo said, then stopped and scratched his head. "But what if the fellow at the other end didn't have his tape recorder set up and waiting?"

"They must have had an appointment. Last night Leppert asked if the other fellow was ready. Then at the end he said, 'Same time tomorrow night.' That means he's going to send another message tonight at eight-fifteen. That's why I borrowed this little machine from Bill Hootner. Tonight I'm going to try and pick up that message."

Bimbo scratched his head again. "Sounds like a great idea," he said. "But how are you going to hook that thing up on Leppert's telephone?"

"I'm not going to try. I'm going to be back in that lavatory again when he sends the message. The desk is only a few feet away, and Leppert plays it pretty loud, so the other tape recorder can pick it up over the telephone. I think this machine can do the same thing if I put the microphone just inside the door."

"They must be sending some pretty confidential stuff to go to all that trouble," Bimbo said.

"That's what I figure."

With the plan for the evening set, the boys turned to other things. Phil explained that he still didn't know about the certificate. His father had come in late the night before and had still been asleep when Phil left that morning. "I didn't have the heart to wake him up," Phil said. "He looks terrible. I'm going to try and get him to see Dr. Calvin."

That evening at eight o'clock, Phil and Bimbo again entered the front door of the city hall. Phil had wondered what Mr. Hansen would say when they came back again, but he didn't have to worry. The old custodian was nowhere in sight. They started down the corridor, but when Phil saw that Leppert's office door was open and that a light was burning inside, he pulled back.

Phil hoped it was Hansen in the office and not Leppert. He doubted that the private secretary was in there. If it were Leppert, he would probably have the door closed. As the minutes dragged by, Phil grew more worried. What if Hansen stayed in the office until Leppert arrived? Phil clutched the compact little tape recorder to his body and waited.

At ten minutes after eight, Jon Hansen came out. He snapped off the lights, closed the door, and shuffled off down the corridor away from the boys. "You stick with Hansen, but don't let him see you," Phil whispered to Bimbo, "I've still got time to get this set up."

Bimbo made a circle with his thumb and forefinger for luck, and the boys started down the corridor together.

Phil had his jacket off by the time he reached Leppert's door, and he had the lid off the tape recorder by the time he was at the desk. Quickly he wrapped the jacket around the case, so that only the reels and the sound heads were exposed. He flipped the switch on and nodded with satisfaction when the jacket muffled the sound of the motor.

Phil set the tape recorder on the floor of the lavatory, plugged in the mike, and adjusted the door so that it was slightly ajar. This left an opening of an inch on the hinge side, and Phil carefully placed the mike on the floor against the opening. Everything was set now.

He wasn't a moment too soon, for he had no more than straightened up when he heard the leather heel clicks coming down the hall. He crouched back down beside the tape recorder and waited. Tonight he wouldn't peek out. He knew what would happen out there in the office.

The routine of the evening before was repeated: the key in the lock of the cabinet, the dialing of the telephone, the question over the phone, and then the quick, garbled message.

Phil had waited until the phone was being dialed before he turned on his own recorder. He had the gain on full to give the mike every chance to pick up the message. His hand trembled as he shut the recorder off and waited. The evening before, Leppert had almost come in the lavatory to wash his hands. Tonight there was the sound of the cabinet being locked, then a silent pause before Phil heard the outside door close. When he heard the staccato heel clicks in the corridor, he breathed a deep sigh of relief.

Phil set the tape recorder on Leppert's desk and put on his jacket. He tenderly lifted the reel of tape off the spindle and held it up, to examine it in the dim light. Here he might have something important, something that would clear his father's name. Or he might have nothing. There was no way of telling until he could play it back at slow speed.

CHAPTER 5

P_{HIL} R_{ELOCKED} the front door of Scotty's
studio after he and Bimbo had entered. Then he set the tape
recorder on the desk and took from his pocket the box with
the tape inside.

"Man, I sure hope you got something," Bimbo said.

Phil removed the lid and dropped the reel down on the
spindle. After a moment, Bimbo stepped up. "Here, let me
thread that thing," he said.

"With your fat fingers?" Phil said derisively.

"At least my fingers aren't trembling."

"I'll get it. You stand back." Phil managed to seat the tape
down in the slot and fasten the end to the take-up reel.
"Here goes," he said and turned on the switch. There was a
silence as the leader ran through before the speaker came to
life with a dragging series of clicks. "That's Leppert dialing
the telephone," Phil said.

"It doesn't sound like a telephone to me."

"I recorded it at high speed. We're playing it back slow."
Then came a drawn out, heavy drawl. "That's Leppert asking the guy if he's ready," Phil said.

"He's sure got a deep voice."

Then another man's voice came from the speaker. The

58

voice was faint, but it could be heard with the volume control turned up. It sounded hollow and faraway, but it was audible.

"This should be the last word you'll have from me for awhile," the voice said.

"That's Mayor Warford's voice," Bimbo said.

Phil held up his hand for silence as the voice continued. "Contact H.O. and tell him everything's under control up here, but to destroy anything that might link me with him on this job. If the authorities question him, have him tell them he'll cooperate, but have him get in touch with me before he makes any statements. King Rooster is swinging public opinion here to our side. We're going to hang the blame on the city engineer because of that variance. The local yokels should go for it big if the campaign is handled right. Tell H.O. to sit tight, and be sure you erase this tape."

There was the dragging growl of Leppert's voice again, but Phil snapped the switch off and the boys looked at each other.

"Man!" Bimbo said in an awed tone. "Did you hear that?"

Phil grinned. "It looks like we got what we went after."

"That was Tom Warford's voice all right. You could recognize the rumble."

Phil nodded. "That's the beauty of it. Everyone will recognize this as Mayor Warford's own voice."

Phil rewound the tape and played it again. Both of them listened intently, trying to pick up anything they might have missed the first time. There was plenty on the tape that he didn't understand, Phil realized, but there was still plenty that he knew would clear his father. Anyone who heard the tape couldn't help but recognize that Warford was deliberately using the variance to frame Mr. Martinson. They had the mayor's confession in his own words.

"Who do you suppose this King Rooster is?" Bimbo said.

Phil had wondered about King Rooster, and he had remembered how Scotty had told them that some people believed there was a power behind the throne here in Seacrest. The real boss could be called King Rooster, but that was something that could be worked out later. "Who's H.O.?" he asked.

Bimbo shook his head. "I don't know any H.O."

"I don't either." Phil took the tape off and placed it in the box. Now that they had this valuable evidence, he was debating with himself on how he could use it. The more citizens of Seacrest who heard Mayor Warford's confession, the better, but he and Bimbo couldn't drag people in off the streets and make them listen. Suddenly he snapped his fingers and whirled. "Bimbo," he said, "you're going to bring your father over here."

Bimbo stared at him. "Me?"

"Samuel Barnes is the most influential man in town. He's the head of the Citizens' Protective League, and if we can sell the League on this, we'll make a copy of the tape and give it to them. They can do a hundred times more good with it than we can alone."

"I guess so," Bimbo said. "Shall I tell him what's on the tape?"

"No," Phil said firmly. "I want him to hear it straight from Mayor Warford's own lips. It's sure to carry more impact that way."

"I'll try," Bimbo said slowly. "I'm not saying he won't come, but to be safe, I think I'll line Mother up on my side. If I can figure out some angle to sell her, I'll guarantee my father will be here."

"I don't care how you swing it, but get him over here to listen to this tape. Have him bring Virgil Charters and any of the other big shots he can drag along."

"All right," Bimbo said weakly. "But why don't you ask Scotty to do it?"

"We can't drag Scotty into it that much. I do want him to hear the tape and give us advice, but you'll have to handle your father."

When Phil arrived home from the studio that night, he found his father at the desk in the corner of the living room, writing checks for the household bills. His father turned in the chair. "Hello, son. You have a good day?"

"Fair." Phil dropped into the easy chair his father usually used. He was glad he had found his father home, for he wanted not only to tell him about the tape, but also to check on the certificate. He waited until his father had closed his checkbook. "I have some good news, Dad," he said.

His father looked at him without smiling. "That would be a change," he said.

Phil had debated with himself which subject to bring up first and now decided to get the business of the certificate out of the way first. "Did you get that slip the inspector signed for the concrete?" he asked.

Carl Martinson stared down at the desk. "No. When I looked for it the next morning, it was gone."

"You mean somebody took it?"

His father looked up with despair in his eyes. "I told you how hopeless it is to try and fight Warford." He shook his head. "If only I had realized how important that paper was at the time. But I didn't, I . . ." His voice trailed off into nothing. It was a shock to Phil to see how his father had lost his will to fight back.

If Phil had heard this news yesterday, it would have been a heavy blow. The certificate would have been a strong piece of evidence, but now with the tape, they had an even stronger weapon. It hurt him, though, to think how easily Warford had duped his father. "How about the inspector who signed the slip? Do you think he'll admit to anything?"

His father still stared down. "He's gone," he said in a choked voice. "There was a note on my desk the next morning, saying he had gone on his vacation. The note said he had gone into Idaho on a hunting trip."

"To stay until this thing blows over," Phil said bitterly. "Did Warford send him away?"

"I suppose so." His father slowly lifted his head. "I told you, son . . ."

"I know what you told me, Dad. But I haven't been sitting still since our talk. I've come up with a surprise for old Warford that'll shake him down to his heels." He looked over at the desk. "Dad, did you allow a variance on that job out there?"

His father stared back blankly. "Yes," he said slowly, "there was a variance—a matter of a couple of inches more span on the rafters than the code calls for."

Phil leaned forward in the chair. "Could that extra span in any way have caused that wall to fall down?"

For the first time that evening Carl Martinson showed a spark of spirit. "No, of course not. If there had been any element of danger, I wouldn't have allowed the variance."

Phil decided to hold off telling his father that the variance was going to be used against him. Instead, he shifted to another tack and told how he and Bimbo had gone to city hall the evening before. He told of his conversation with Jon Hansen and how he had hidden in the lavatory.

Mr. Martinson frowned and reached out his hand. "You mean you entered the man's office? You searched his desk and then eavesdropped?"

Phil had never thought whether what he had done was morally right or not. Now his father's rebuke made him angry. "Good grief! This bunch of crooks stole stuff out of *your* desk. They've lied about you. They're accusing you of things you never did. They've even caused the death of a good friend of yours, and you're worrying about whether it's wrong to eavesdrop to get evidence against them."

Carl Martinson stroked the side of his face with a bewildered motion. "I don't know," he said feebly, "I don't know. Everything's wrong—maybe I'm wrong. I must have done something wrong, somewhere."

A feeling of compassion welled up in Phil. He got out of the chair, walked over, and put his arm across his father's shoulders. It was his first outward display of affection toward him, yet Phil did not feel embarrassed. "When you hear how things turned out, maybe you'll forgive me, Dad."

His father kept his head bowed while Phil explained the

taping of the coded message in Leppert's office. Then as best he could remember, he recited what Mayor Warford had said in the message.

His father looked up with a wan smile. "I was wrong," he said. "I didn't know enough to fight fire with fire."

Phil patted his father's shoulder and walked over to the chair. When he looked back, he saw that Mr. Martinson now sat up straight—the defeatist slump was gone. Phil searched around for a new angle to attack the problem. "Who is the contractor on that job, Dad?"

"Osterly," his father said. "Herman Osterly."

Something clicked in Phil's brain when he heard the name. He spoke it aloud, then slammed his hand down on the chair arm. "That's it!" he shouted. "H.O.—Herman Osterly. The contractor was the one Warford was talking about in the message. That proves Osterly and Warford are in cahoots on this thing."

Phil had promised to return the borrowed tape recorder the next morning, so he went to the studio early, hoping to play the tape for Scotty before he took the recorder back to Bill Hootner. He was waiting impatiently when the phone rang. It was Scotty saying he had a bad toothache and would go to the dentist before he came to the studio.

Bimbo walked in while Phil was still sunk down in the chair behind the desk. He listened to Phil tell about Scotty's call, then said, "At least I've got some good news. My father's going to come over and listen, but it took a family uprising to get him to agree. I had Mother all primed, so when he started in on me, she told him he was arresting my intellectual development and retarding my inquisitive instincts.

That's something she's read in a book," Bimbo explained. "Anyway, he finally gave in."

"Good. Is he going to bring Virgil Charters?"

"It set him off again when I asked him to do that," Bimbo said. "But Mother told him Mr. Charters would be glad to cooperate in my intellectual development. He finally gave in on that, too."

"When are they coming?"

"He said he would talk to Charters today, and they would come in tomorrow morning."

Phil was disappointed. He had hoped he could give the demonstration at once. This way Mayor Warford would have another full day in which to spread his propaganda. He realized his face must have showed his disappointment. "You did a good job, Bimbo," he said, forcing a smile.

"Mother did the job."

Phil went over to the wooden cabinet against the wall where Scotty kept his negative file. He turned the key in the lock and swung the door open. Inside, there were rows of vertical partitions, and he reached over to the end of a shelf where he had put the box containing the tape recording. "Still safe and sound," he said and carried it back to the machine.

Phil wanted to hear the message once more himself. Again he listened to each word Warford said, and when the message was over, he turned off the machine and replaced the lid. He still had no idea who King Rooster was, but now that he knew that H.O. was the contractor, the message made more sense. For one thing, Warford wanted the contractor to destroy anything that would link the mayor with the faulty building; another was that the man was to pretend to co-operate with any investigation.

Phil replaced the tape in the cabinet and locked the door. He had Bimbo return the tape recorder as promised. He intended to borrow it again the next morning, and he wanted to stay on the good side of Bill Hootner.

Scotty came into the office around eleven, and Phil told him about the tape. He took it from the cabinet and explained why the recorder had been returned. Scotty listened soberly while Phil told him what the tape contained. When Phil finished, Scotty stroked his jaw. "You're on dangerous ground there," he said.

"I've got the evidence against Mayor Warford," Phil said stubbornly.

"That's not legal evidence, Phil. That tape couldn't be used in court."

"I don't think this is ever going to get to court," Phil replied. "I want the people in town to hear this. I want them to hear how Warford is framing my father."

Scotty drew his eyebrows together. "You don't think Tom Warford and his bunch are going to take this lying down?"

"I don't know what they can do about it," Phil said hotly. Scotty's critical attitude, even before he had heard the tape, annoyed him. He was about to retort that he hoped the Citizens' Protective League would be more receptive, when Scotty walked over to his desk and flipped up the page on his appointment book.

"We're going out to Astro Electronics this afternoon," he said abruptly. "They want pictures for a brochure. We'll take the view camera and all the lighting equipment. You'd better load the stuff into the station wagon right away."

The job at Astro Electronics took a great deal of careful lighting. Phil set the floodlights and spots up in the drafting room and then took innumerable light meter readings at different points. At the best, this was tedious work, and when Scotty refused to be satisfied with any light setup he made, Phil grew irritated. He wished the afternoon was over.

After two hours of work, they had taken only two shots, and neither of them had satisfied Scotty. Phil was returning from another trip to the station wagon when Scotty stepped in front of him. Scotty stood with his hands planted on his hips and glared. "What did I send you for?" he demanded. "A reflector, or a skrim?"

Phil looked down at the cheesecloth-covered frame he held in his hand. "A reflector, I guess," he mumbled. "I'm sorry."

Things seemed to go that way all afternoon, so Phil was glad when it was five o'clock. He stacked the lights against the wall and followed Scotty out of the building. He had wanted Scotty to be at the demonstration the next morning when Samuel Barnes and the others came to the studio. Now he hesitated to ask his boss. He loaded the gear into the wagon and came back around. He took a deep breath and asked Scotty if he would stay the next day to hear the tape.

Scotty climbed into the front seat without replying. He sat behind the wheel and frowned. "We have a job to finish here."

"I know," Phil protested. "But this is so important. That tape we have could save my father."

"I hope you're not building your hopes too high on that tape recording," Scotty said. He drummed his fingers on the wheel. "You're not playing with a bunch of kids. Those are dangerous men, and they know how to play rough." Scotty reached down and turned on the ignition switch. "I'll be there," he said.

Bill Hootner opened his camera shop himself, and Phil was waiting on the sidewalk when Hootner appeared to unlock his place at nine. Phil picked up the same recorder he had used before and hurried over to the photo studio, hoping to be able to play the tape through at least once before the others arrived.

Scotty was in the office. He sat behind his desk, his pipe in his mouth, and his face relaxed. He watched Phil unlock the cabinet and take out the tape. Phil took the lid off, but had no more than placed the reel on the spindle when the door opened and a man strode in.

Bimbo's father, Samuel Barnes, was a tall, hawk-nosed, scowling man whose clothes hung loosely on his rawboned frame. He glared around the room. His glare slid over Phil and settled on Scotty. "Are you a party to this ridiculous affair, Kendall?"

Scotty grinned. "I'm only an innocent bystander, Sam."

Mr. Barnes stepped aside and a chubby little man with pink cheeks came in and stood beside him. "Good morning, Phillip," he said.

"Good morning, Mr. Charters."

Scotty grinned when Virgil Charters looked at him. "Don't ask me if I know what's going on, Virgil," he said. "I haven't heard it myself."

Phil saw a third man enter—a tall, well-dressed, younger man. He knew this was Melton Flood. Flood worked for Samuel Barnes and was being groomed to be manager of Barnes Department Store. He was also a member of the Citizens' League, but Phil thought that might be to impress his boss. Flood stepped back against the wall, folded his arms across his chest, and regarded Phil with an indulgent smile.

Bimbo slipped into the office and closed the door behind him.

Phil cleared his throat. "I'm not going to make a speech," he said. "I only want you men to listen to this tape recording with an open mind, then decide." His fingers seemed even more clumsy than they had been the other evening when he tried to thread the tape into the machine. He was conscious of the eyes on him. Finally, he secured the end of the tape to the take-up reel and stepped back. "Listen to this," he said and snapped on the switch.

The reels turned slowly. Phil felt a shiver run through his body as he waited for the sound of the telephone being dialed, the sound that came before Leppert would speak. Phil watched the machine closely; the leader must be almost through. The take-up reel was filling with tape, but still there was only silence from the speaker. Phil knew the message should be on now. Frantically he flipped the switch off and on again. The machine ground the tape through the slot without so much as a whisper.

Phil glanced up and saw Bimbo's stricken expression. He heard someone cough impatiently.

He ran the tape back and plugged in the microphone. "Testing," he said hoarsely into the mike. "Testing, one-two-three." He ran the tape back, then forward again. "Testing," the speaker said in a hoarse voice. "Testing, one-two-three." Then there was only silence.

Melton Flood unfolded his arms. "So this is what we took time off to hear," he said.

Mr. Barnes glared at Phil. Then he turned to glare at Bimbo. "You young nimcompoop," he yelled. "You . . . you . . ." He raised his arms.

Bimbo backed away. "Remember my intellectual development, Father," he said weakly.

"You don't have any development. You don't have any intellect!"

"Remember Mother."

"Why I ever let her talk me into this ridiculous . . ."

"Now, Sam," Charters said soothingly, "don't be too hard on the boy. He evidently thought he had something to show us, or he wouldn't have asked you to come over here."

Melton Flood stepped up to stand beside Samuel Barnes. "This may be some kind of a boyish prank," he said, "but I fail to see the point."

Phil took his eyes from the tape recorder to look behind the desk. Scotty was puffing on his pipe, and it was impossible for Phil to tell whether or not the man was concerned. Phil turned to Bimbo's father. "I'm sorry, Mr. Barnes," he said. "There was a voice on that tape. It was Mayor Warford's voice. I'll swear there was."

"Where is that voice now?" Flood asked sarcastically.

"I don't know."

"I thought not!" Samuel Barnes yelled.

"Now, Sam," Charters said again, "there's been no real harm done. We . . ."

"No real harm? You can talk, you don't have a business that goes to rack and ruin when you're not there." Mr. Barnes turned on Bimbo. He raised his fists and waved them helplessly in the air. "Wait until I talk to your mother," he shouted and stomped out, with Melton Flood close on his heels.

"I'm sorry things turned out this way," Virgil Charters said to Scotty. He followed the others through the door.

Phil watched the men leave. Slowly he turned to look helplessly at Scotty. "There was a voice on that tape," he said. "Bimbo will tell you there was."

"Sure there was," Bimbo said. "It was Mayor Warford's voice."

Scotty placed his pipe in the ash tray and stood up. "Remember what I told you out at the plant yesterday afternoon?" he said to Phil.

"But we had it on the tape," Phil protested. "Why shouldn't I get my hopes high? It was Warford's own voice. He said that they were going to hang the blame on the city engineer. He said the local yokels would go for it big if the campaign was handled right."

"You've got to have that in Warford's own voice." He bunched his eyebrows at Phil. "No, son," he said, "it looks like your big exposé of Mayor Warford has turned out to be nothing but a big bust."

CHAPTER 6

SCOTTY was sympathetic when he saw how utterly crushed Phil was over the blank tape, and he suggested that Phil take the rest of the day off. "You'd be less help to me today than you were yesterday," he said with a wry grin. "Go off somewhere and try to forget it."

Phil couldn't forget what had happened. He and Bimbo were still stunned when they carried the tape recorder back to the camera shop.

Bill Hootner, a quiet, gray-haired man, listened to Phil's story of the tape. "Are you sure this is the same tape that had the voice on it?" he asked.

"Yes," Phil said wearily, "I nicked it the other night when I threaded it up. The nick is still there."

"The tape has been erased then. If you're sure you didn't accidentally erase it yourself . . ."

"I didn't," Phil said. "I played it yesterday, then put it in the box, and put the box in the file cabinet."

"The cabinet was locked," Bimbo said.

Bill Hootner stared at the ceiling for some time. "Sound is put on tape by magnetic impulses," he finally said. "To make it blank again, you demagnetize the tape." He went on to explain how a demagnetizer sets up a field and how any tape brought into the field is erased. To demonstrate his point, Hootner brought out a small, round piece of equipment. He explained that when the cord was plugged into a wall socket, a strong demagnetizing field was set up. "This is a bulk eraser," he said. "It will erase a whole reel of tape at one time."

"Would that field penetrate a piece of wood, say half an inch thick?" Phil asked as an idea began to form in his mind.

"Oh, yes."

The idea was taking shape now, and Phil asked more questions. Bill Hootner told him that the field extended as far as three feet from the eraser, but that it had to be brought within a few inches to do an effective job. Phil remembered now how he had placed the tape upright, within inches of the outside cabinet wall. "Are there many of these bulk erasers around?" he asked.

"Since hi-fi is so popular, a lot of people own tape recorders," he said. "Some of them have these bulk erasers. You could buy one at any store that carries a large stock."

Phil thanked Bill Hootner for the use of the recorder and left. Outside he heaved a deep sigh. "I guess you know what must have happened, Bimbo."

"I think so," Bimbo said, "but fill me in on the details."

"Let's go over to the malt shop. It might go down easier along with a fudge sundae."

In the booth, Bimbo looked down at the dish before him. "Your idea of a fudge sundae was swell," he said.

"It was pretty simple," Phil said, staring at a point over Bimbo's head. "Somebody knew where the tape was. They brought in a bulk eraser, put it against the outside of the cabinet, and erased our tape."

"But the only person who was in the office . . ." Bimbo stopped.

"It didn't have to be somebody in the office," Phil said quickly. "Whoever did it could have broken in last night."

"Maybe so," Bimbo said, "but it had to be somebody who knew that we had the tape and that it was in the office."

Phil went back over all that had happened since he had recorded the tape in Leppert's office. He counted each person off on his fingers that could have known. There were himself and Bimbo. There were Bimbo's father and mother. "Did you tell your folks where the tape was?"

"I might have," Bimbo admitted. "I guess I did."

Phil went on with his counting. There was Virgil Charters, Melton Flood, and Scotty. There was his own father, and he had no idea who his father or the others might have told. When he had eight fingers up, he slumped down and groaned.

"I don't get it," Bimbo said, holding his spoon in mid-air. "Why would anyone go to all the trouble of using a bulk eraser? If it was Scotty, he could have unlocked the cabinet and swiped the tape. If somebody broke in, why didn't they go ahead and break into the cabinet and take the whole thing with them?"

Phil had been wondering the same thing. He had mulled it over until he thought he had an answer. "Look," he said, "suppose we had found the cabinet open and the tape gone. What would we have done?"

"We'd holler that we'd been robbed."

"Right, and if we insisted that we had the evidence against Warford and that the evidence had been stolen, at least some of the people would have listened. Most people like to think the worst. Look how they believe that stuff about Dad. A robbery would have aroused suspicion against Warford around town. At least there would have been talk, and Warford doesn't want that right now."

"That makes sense," Bimbo agreed.

"But Mayor Warford's bunch are smart. They don't do anything crude, like stealing the tape. They quietly erase our evidence and make us look like a couple of saps. They let us go ahead and hang ourselves in front of the leaders of the Citizens' League. Now they'll never believe us again."

Bimbo looked woeful. "I'm glad you told me this when I was eating," he said. "Otherwise I think I'd be sick."

Phil remembered how sure his father had been that Warford would be too clever for them. He also knew Scotty had warned him of the same thing. Now he winced when he realized that Mayor Warford had defeated him with more ease than he had Carl Martinson. "I sure hate to tell Dad what happened," Phil said. "I built him so high on this thing last night, and he's had so many disappointments lately. I feel terrible."

"So do I. I think I'll have Gracie bring me a refill."

Phil thought of how broken his father had seemed the evening before. Now, instead of building him up, he had helped to tear down what reserve strength the man had left. "I think we should go over to the studio and have a look around," he told Bimbo. "Maybe we can find out whether anyone really did break into the place."

The boys made sure the front door of Scotty's studio hadn't been tampered with. Then they went around to the back. The rear door was locked with a spring catch, and it looked as if the door had been pried back enough to allow a thin strip to be inserted to push the spring catch back.

"It wasn't an inside job, anyway," Bimbo said.

"Why?" Phil demanded. "If you had pulled an inside job, wouldn't you try to make it look like it wasn't an inside job?"

The boys went back into the office and sat in glum silence, glaring at the cabinet. As Phil thought back over Warford's message, the name "King Rooster" stuck in his mind. That was the one part that still hadn't been cleared up. From the way the mayor had spoken, King Rooster was one of the local citizens. That would mean he could be someone they had trusted.

Phil heaved a sigh and settled down again. King Rooster could have been the one who had betrayed him and Bimbo by tipping off their plans to Mayor Warford. If this was so, King Rooster was even more dangerous than Warford himself. They still didn't know who King Rooster was, so there was no way to fight him. But they did know that the mayor was their enemy. Phil looked up when Bimbo climbed out of his chair.

"I think I'd better go home and swing Mother over to my side again," Bimbo said. "I'm going to need all the help I can get when my father gets home tonight."

Phil lifted his hand listlessly in farewell as Bimbo walked out.

It was some time before Phil could force himself into action. He decided to go out to the building once more. He would take a camera and shoot some close-up shots of that wall. A picture might show up flaws in the concrete.

On the way out to Ramona Road, Phil's enthusiasm rose. Pictures of that wall could be valuable evidence. He wondered why he hadn't thought of it before. He knew why he hadn't thought of it—he had been so concerned with that tape recording, he had overlooked every other angle.

This time Phil parked out on the road. He had brought his own 35mm camera, and he shoved it into his jacket pocket as he climbed out and started across the open space. Phil frowned when he saw the building and the number of men working. He had thought they would leave the wall as it was until there had been an investigation. It had been only four days since the accident, but already there were new forms up on that side.

He stopped inside the door opening. There was not a scrap of the old wall left; a whole new side of the building was going up in its place. He looked up to see a squat, dark-complexioned man in a metal protective helmet coming toward him.

"What are you looking for?" the man demanded when he was still twenty feet away.

Phil looked around for the big man he had talked to on the day of the accident. "I want to talk to the foreman," he said.

"I'm the foreman," the man growled. "What's your business?"

"I'm a photographer." Phil had his camera halfway out of his pocket when a hairy paw grabbed his wrist and twisted.

"Get out of here!" the man shouted. "Get out!"

The twist had wrenched Phil's hand off the camera, and

he braced himself against being pushed. Over the dark man's shoulder, he saw two more men stop work and start toward them. "I'm not hurting anything," Phil said.

"This is private property. Get out of here, or we'll throw you off."

"You'd better go while you can still walk," one of the other men said.

Phil held his ground for a moment against the advancing men. He was no match for the three of them, and besides, there was nothing left to take pictures of now. "Take it easy," he said. "I'm leaving."

The workmen followed him to the doorway and watched him cross the open space. Phil was angry with himself. He had missed the boat again by not taking pictures of that wall when he had the chance. Osterly hadn't wasted any time. He would tear out every bit of faulty concrete now, and Phil knew that when the new walls went up, they would meet all specifications.

Phil talked to his father in the living room before dinner. He watched carefully as he told him about the blank tape. His father's face muscles sagged a bit more, but other than that he showed no emotion. "That's too bad, son. I'm sorry."

Phil told him about his trip to the building. "Don't you know what they're doing, Dad? Can't you stop them?"

His father closed his eyes. "Mayor Warford is the authority in this town. They won't allow me near that building."

Anger filled Phil when he thought how his father was being shoved around. Of course, it was by Mayor Warford's orders that the city engineer was being kept away, but they

couldn't prove it. His father couldn't appeal to the police—
the police belonged to the mayor. Phil was about to burst
into a tirade against Warford, when Mrs. Flemming called
them in to dinner.

Phil and his father ate in silence. Mrs. Flemming kept up
her chatter, but Phil had learned to catch only key words
that would give him the trend of her monologue. Halfway
through the meal he heard, "town forum," and "tomorrow
night." "What forum is that?" he asked.

Mrs. Flemming never minded repeating herself. "Why,
the public forum meeting tomorrow night at the civic auditorium," she said. "Mayor Warford is going to answer questions from the stage."

Phil turned to his father. "Did you know anything about
this?"

His father nodded. "There's quite a bit of talk about it
down at city hall."

"If Mayor Warford is on the stage, the thing's rigged,"
Phil said.

"Oh, no," Mrs. Flemming said. "This is all going to be very
fair and honest. It's quite educational, too. The Women's
Club of Seacrest is sponsoring it. Mrs. Barnes is very civic-
minded, you know."

"Mrs. Barnes? You mean, Bimbo's mother?"

Mrs. Flemming beamed. "Yes, she's running the whole
thing, I guess. She's the president of the Women's Club, you
know. Of course I don't belong myself, but I do hear what
goes on, and if I do say so, she . . ."

"Dad," Phil said, "you don't think this thing's going to be
on the level, do you?"

"I don't know," his father said cautiously. "I'd hesitate to think that Mrs. Barnes would do anything dishonest."

"As president of the Women's Club," Mrs. Flemming began, "Mrs. Barnes . . ."

"I don't think she would do anything crooked," Phil said. "But Warford could plant stooges out there in the audience to ask him the questions he wanted to answer."

"I suppose he could," his father said.

"I know Mrs. Barnes will make quite a thing of this forum," Mrs. Flemming said. "She always does when she . . ."

"Are you going, Dad?"

His father looked down at his plate. "No, son, I'm not."

Phil realized how his father must feel. The questions asked at the forum would concern the building accident and the death of Victor Sanchez. There would be accusations made, both from the floor and the stage, against the city engineer's office. Phil knew that his father wasn't capable of standing up and defending himself in public. "I think I'll go to that meeting," Phil said. "That is, if you don't object, Dad."

His father shook his head slowly. "I won't forbid you to go. You're not a child any longer. You'll have to make your own decisions in a matter of this kind."

"Oh, I'm sure it will be a very nice event, Mr. Martinson. Everything that Mrs. Barnes puts on . . ."

"I'm sure it will be very nice, Mrs. Flemming. Now, if you'll excuse me . . ."

Bimbo came over later, and Phil took him up to his room. He closed the door and turned. "Why didn't you tell me about this meeting your mother has cooked up?" he demanded.

Bimbo looked owl-eyed. "Huh?"

"This public forum at the civic auditorium tomorrow night. Your mother's running the thing."

"She is? Maybe I'd better pay more attention to what's going on around home. What's a public forum, anyway?"

Phil explained how any person in the audience could ask questions of the speaker. "In this case, Warford will use the forum as a sounding board for his propaganda," Phil said. "He'll have the audience loaded with plants. They'll ask the questions he wants to answer, and he'll evade the questions that might put him on the spot."

"That sounds about what Warford would pull," Bimbo said glumly. "He'll have a ball."

"Not if I can help it. Bimbo, we're going to that meeting to ask a few questions of our own. We're going to see that Warford answers them straight, too."

"*We're* going?"

"All right, you don't have to go if you don't want to."

"I'll go, but I don't know whether they'll let you in or not," Bimbo said.

"It's a public forum," Phil explained patiently. "I'm part of the public. They can't keep me out."

"I don't know. My mother's club does some pretty weird things sometimes."

"You let me worry about that," Phil said. "Now we're going to have to dress up, wear our suits and ties. We're going to be gentlemen and not act wise. We don't want to make the audience sore at us. We want them to be on our side.

We'll stand up, request the floor, and then ask our questions politely. No matter how Warford riles us, we can't lose our tempers."

"That's going to be tough," Bimbo said.

"Of course it is. Anyone can stand up and yell, but that doesn't put your point over. The best way is to ask straight questions, and if Warford hedges, the audience will know there's something wrong."

"It could turn out to be a pretty interesting evening," Bimbo said thoughtfully. "I guess I could be a gentleman for a couple of hours."

"There's something that's been bothering me, Bimbo," Phil said. "I want to find out who suggested this public forum in the first place. I want to know if Mayor Warford cooked it up." The setup seemed too pat to Phil. He didn't believe that Mrs. Barnes and her club were working for the mayor, but then they could have been used as dupes to sponsor something Warford couldn't do under his own name. Phil was determined to be more careful this time. "Don't even tell your father you're going to this forum," he told Bimbo.

"I wouldn't get the chance. I've had a break so far. My father didn't come home this evening—he had a Chamber of Commerce dinner downtown. I think I'll stay out of his way until that thing this morning blows over."

The boys went back over all the events that had happened since the building accident. They talked about the tape message and wondered if King Rooster might show his hand at the meeting. It was almost ten o'clock when Bimbo left.

Phil went into the living room, where his father sat slumped in the chair, staring at the wall. The evening newspaper lay folded and unnoticed in his lap. He looked up slowly as Phil spoke.

"Dad, did you mention that tape Bimbo and I had to any-one?"

His father's eyes remained blank. "Yes," he finally said in a low voice, "I mentioned it to Jon Hansen. I thought he knew you had slipped back into Leppert's office."

"He didn't," Phil said curtly.

"So he told me. Jon was very upset over what you had done."

Phil thought he knew why the custodian was upset, and he couldn't bring himself to censure his father for telling Hansen. Phil hoped the tape wouldn't cause the custodian any trouble, and he knew he would have to go down to city hall and try to appease the old man. "I'll apologize to Mr. Hansen," he said. He studied his father's haggard face. "Why don't you go upstairs and go to bed, Dad? You need sleep."

"Sleep comes hard these nights. When you're my age, you can't shrug these things off anymore." He raised his hand and made a futile gesture. "I don't know—I just don't seem to know how to cope with it."

Phil put his hand on his father's shoulder. "Try to get some rest," he said. "We're going to work everything out fine—together."

CHAPTER 7

THE NEXT EVENING Bimbo called and asked Phil to pick him up at the malt shop. Bimbo was waiting, dressed in his best suit, when Phil pulled up to the curb. "We had bread pudding for dinner tonight," Bimbo said, coming up to the car. "I had to stop in here for dessert." He looked at Phil. "Man, we look like a couple of pallbearers on their way to a big job."

"I hope we're going to Warford's political funeral," Phil said, swinging the door open. "Get in, you'll attract a crowd standing out there."

As he drove to the civic auditorium, Phil again emphasized the importance of being gentlemen at the meeting. "We have to act serious if we expect the audience to take us seriously," he said.

"Even with this tie choking me, I'll be serious," Bimbo said. "As I succumb, I promise to sink slowly to the floor with a serious expression on my youthful and handsome face."

"Just don't try to be a comedian when we get there." Phil had come early, as he wanted to get seats in the center section well down in front. He parked in the parking lot, and as they walked back down the sidewalk, Phil saw that a few people had already started to trickle into the auditorium.

Ahead of them, at the side of the building, a dark passageway ran down to the stage door at the rear. A uniformed policeman stepped from the passageway and stopped them. "Was either of you fellows ever a Boy Scout?" he asked.

"We both were," Bimbo said.

"Would you mind giving me a hand then?" The policeman walked back down the passageway. At the stage door, he went in and beckoned for the boys to follow. They walked behind him, down a corridor. "Hey, what gives here?" Bimbo whispered.

Phil was walking ahead of Bimbo. "I don't know, maybe . . ." With the sentence half-finished, Phil was grabbed by someone who had stepped out of a doorway. He was spun around and jammed against the wall.

"Get your hands against that wall," a voice barked. Phil half turned, and got a stiff jolt in the back that straightened him up with a cry of pain. "I said hands against the wall," the voice said again.

With his hands braced against the concrete, Phil turned his head to see Bimbo in the same position beside him. He felt rough but expert hands run over his body in a quick search. A hand plunged into his side coat pocket and held there. "I hit pay dirt," the voice said.

"Me, too," another voice said behind Bimbo. "OK, you birds, turn around."

Phil turned and saw a tall and a short man, both in civilian clothes. He looked down the corridor. The uniformed policeman had disappeared. "Who are you?" he demanded.

"Police," the tall man said, but made no move to produce identification.

"Police?" Phil said. "What did you grab us for?"

"Attempted malicious mischief," the tall man said in a flat voice. "We got you dead to rights."

"You've got the wrong fellows. We haven't done anything. A policeman outside asked us if we were ever Boy Scouts, and then he told us to follow him in here." Phil stopped when he realized how ridiculous his story sounded.

"I found these in your pocket." The tall man held out his hand to display six glass vials, each filled with an amber fluid. "They're stink bombs," he said.

The short man held out his hand, and there were six vials in his palm, too. "We caught you sneaking around back here, looking for the ventilating system."

Phil was bewildered. He tried to make some sense out of the swift-moving chain of events. One moment he and Bimbo had been up on the street, minding their business, and the next thing he knew they had been charged with malicious mischief. There was something terribly wrong. At first he thought someone must have planted those things in his and Bimbo's pockets and then notified the police. Phil didn't doubt that these plainclothesmen were police.

Then it hit him between the eyes. They were police, but whose police? They belonged to Mayor Warford. Those stink bombs had been planted in his pockets all right—but they had been planted by the plainclothesmen. "Look," Phil said hotly, "you put those things in my pocket."

"Get them out of the hall," the short man said.

"Get in that room," the tall man said, guiding Phil toward an open door.

Phil braced himself, and as he started to turn, he caught a blow over the kidney that almost paralyzed him. "Cut that out," he heard Bimbo say as he stumbled through the door.

The room was a dressing room, with only a make-up table, two straight chairs, and a longer table against the wall. The tall man carried the chairs over to the wall. "You kids sit down there," he ordered.

Phil lowered himself into the chair. The stabbing pain still racked his body. Bimbo sat down beside him and glared at the men. "I'll bet you guys aren't really cops," he said.

"They're cops," Phil said. "Warford's cops." He leaned over and spoke in a low voice. "Don't buck them," he said. "They'd like nothing better than to belt us around for resisting arrest. They're the law, and there's nothing we can do about it." He looked up at the tall man. "If we're being charged with malicious mischief, why don't you take us down to the station?"

"The mayor has a theory on juvenile delinquency. He figures that what you kids need is a little understanding, so he won't treat you like common criminals. He'll talk to you later." The tall policeman walked over to the table. He was joined by his partner, and the two of them talked in low tones, ignoring the boys.

"Man, what a mess," Bimbo whispered. "How do you suppose we ever got tangled up in this?"

"By underestimating Mayor Warford and his bunch again," Phil whispered viciously. "They blocked our plan completely and made us look like a couple of rowdies before

we ever got to the auditorium. They were waiting for us and
. . ." Phil stopped and glared at Bimbo. "Did you tell your
father you were coming here tonight?"

"No, you told me not to. I didn't tell anybody but Mother
. . . I had to tell her," Bimbo added quickly. "If she had
seen me dressed up, she'd have thought something was
wrong."

Phil glowered down at his hands. He knew he couldn't
blame Bimbo too much, even though Mrs. Barnes had probably told Bimbo's father. Phil himself had talked in front of
Mrs. Flemming, and once Mrs. Flemming got on the phone,
she could be a human broadcasting station. He realized that
any number of persons could have tipped off Mayor Warford. There wasn't much sense in trying to put the finger on
one. There were so few people in Seacrest he could really
trust, and it was impossible to keep his plans from everybody. This could be another of King Rooster's betrayals. Phil
started back over the list again, but gave up in disgust.

Phil heard a polite flutter of applause from the auditorium. It made him wince. He could imagine Mayor Warford standing on the stage, a pillar of clean administration,
while he and Bimbo were being held prisoners under Warford's orders.

"What do you suppose they're going to do to us?" Bimbo
said in a hoarse voice.

"I don't know and I don't care. I'm not really worried
about that, Bimbo."

"Well, I am," Bimbo whispered back. "If we get a criminal
record, it could murder our school chances."

Phil understood Bimbo's concern. Bimbo had staked his

future when he had agreed to help Phil. "I'm sorry," Phil said.

"What do you suppose Warford's saying out there?" Bimbo asked.

Phil was grateful that Bimbo hadn't made anything of his apology. "He's telling them how my father's to blame for that accident and how his own administration is lily-white."

For well over an hour Phil was sunk in dejected silence while the plainclothesmen talked in low tones at the table. From time to time there was a smattering of applause from the auditorium. The hot flush of anger left Phil, and despondency took its place. He had failed his father again. This time he hadn't been too cocksure. Yet, Warford had defeated him. There didn't seem to be any way he could hope to beat the mayor. Anyway, he thought, the worst part of this episode is over.

Finally there was a rap at the door. The tall man walked over, opened it, and talked briefly to someone outside. "Come on," he said to the boys. "The meeting's over."

Phil pulled himself to his feet and went out into the hall. "Mission accomplished," he said bitterly. "I suppose you're going to turn us loose now that it's too late for us to ask the mayor any questions." He started forward, but slammed abruptly into the wall when the tall man gave him a hard shove. "Hey!" Phil cried, turning to face the man.

The plainclothesman grabbed Phil's coat and yanked it down over the shoulders, tearing a button off. He twisted Phil's tie to one side, then ripped his shirt collar open. "Giving me trouble, eh?" the man growled. He rumpled Phil's hair and stepped back. "I guess you're ready to make an appearance," he said.

Phil took his comb out, and had it jerked from his hand by the tall man, who pushed him toward the far end of the corridor. Phil and Bimbo were taken through a short hallway and were brought out into the auditorium. A few stragglers turned to stare.

The plainclothesmen marched Phil and Bimbo up the aisle and out through the door, into the lobby, which was still well filled. People were standing in groups, chatting, but when the procession made its entrance, a sudden silence hit Phil like a shock wave.

The tall man took Phil's arm and guided him up to a group. "I'm sorry, your honor," the man said, "but I think I have something that needs your attention."

Mayor Warford swung his large head around to look at them. "What have we here?" he asked with just the right amount of heartiness in his tone to make his question sound sincere. Mayor Warford always used his size, his handsome appearance, and his stentorian voice to great advantage.

"We ran into a little trouble," the tall man said. "We caught these boys slipping around backstage." He indicated Phil. "This one gave us the real trouble," he added.

"Regrettable," the mayor rumbled. He shook his head as he regarded Phil. "What were you doing back there, son?"

Phil knew what kind of an appearance he must make, and he ran his fingers through his rumpled hair. He realized he would have to choose his words carefully, and even then he was afraid he would be no match for the mayor. "We weren't doing anything," he said carefully. "We were . . ."

"I found these in his pocket," the tall man broke in. He held out the glass vials. "Those are stink bombs, your honor. If they had put them into the ventilating system, it would have run everybody out of the auditorium."

The indignant buzz that swept across the lobby made Phil want to crawl down into his clothes. He felt his face redden and knew this would be taken for a sign of guilt. He lowered his head and glared at the floor. He fixed his eyes on Mayor Warford's feet. The mayor wore a pair of highly polished alligator shoes. Phil had never seen alligator shoes on a man before, and he concentrated on these in an effort to shut out the crowd around him.

A tall, stately woman pushed through the crowd and brushed by Phil. "Buford," she said, stopping before Bimbo, "is this true?"

"No, Mother," Bimbo began, "you see . . ."

"Is this young man your son, Mrs. Barnes?" the mayor said in a shocked voice.

"Yes, this is my son Buford."

The mayor clucked his tongue. "An unfortunate occurrence," he rumbled. "But it's an old story. The son of a respectable family becoming involved with bad companions."

"Buford is in the midst of his intellectual development," Mrs. Barnes said, turning to glare at Phil.

"It wasn't Phil's fault," Bimbo said stoutly. "Mother, I'm sorry, but . . ."

"Sorry?" Samuel Barnes shouted, pushing his way up. "Is that all you've got to say for yourself?"

"Mr. Barnes," Mayor Warford said sternly, "your son has already admitted his guilt and has expressed his . . ."

"I didn't admit any guilt," Bimbo said hotly. "When I said I was sorry, I meant . . ."

"I think I realize Buford's position," Warford said, raising his voice. "He feels a certain loyalty to his friend, although that loyalty may be misplaced."

"You're crazy," Bimbo said. "I didn't . . ."

"Quiet!" Samuel Barnes shouted.

The tall man took Phil's arm. "What shall I do with this one, your honor?"

The mayor fixed his eye on Phil, and waited until the silence around him was complete. "What is your name, young man?"

Phil was sure Warford knew his name. He drew himself up and glared. "My name is Phillip Martinson," he said, "and my father is the city engineer." Phil knew the crowd now thought he had come here to break up the meeting, so Mayor Warford couldn't speak against his father. He wanted to turn on them and shout that his father was innocent, that they were being duped by Warford, that this was all part of a big swindle.

Phil fought his temper down and clenched his fists as he faced the mayor. He couldn't trust his voice, even to deny the charge against him. Warford wanted him to deny the charge, Warford wanted him to lose his temper—that was all part of the plan to make Phil Martinson look bad. He remained silent.

Mayor Warford turned away from Phil to face the crowd. "We all recognize the seriousness of the juvenile delinquency problem," he said in his best campaign voice. "As your mayor, I have been deeply concerned. But since this act of vandalism was directed toward me personally, I feel I can temper justice with mercy in this case without criticism." He turned his head slowly to look at Phil. "You may go now, son," he said quietly.

Phil turned and walked stiffly to the front entrance. The crowd parted as a dead hush settled down on the lobby. He walked down the sidewalk in a blind rage, looking to neither the right nor the left. He heard footsteps gaining on him from behind, but he refused to turn around.

When the footsteps were beside him, Scotty Kendall's voice spoke. "Go over to the office," he said. "I want to talk to you."

Phil gave no sign that he had heard, but turned into the parking lot, walked to his car, and did as he was told. He was slumped in a chair with his head bowed when Scotty entered the office. Slowly Phil got to his feet. He had made up his mind not to beg. He would tell what happened, and if Scotty fired him, he would take it without making any protest. They could pile it on, but they weren't going to make him whimper. "I suppose you heard what Warford said in the lobby," he said quietly.

Scotty walked over to his desk and picked up his pipe. "I heard. What is your side of the story?"

Phil explained how he and Bimbo had been lured backstage by the policeman and how they had been held captive by the police. "I was roughed up and pushed out there in front of all those people," he said. "You can imagine how I felt." He told his story simply and then stopped. He wasn't going to plead to be understood.

Scotty tamped tobacco into his pipe. "That was quite an act Warford put on," he said.

Phil looked up suddenly. "You believe me?"

Scotty smiled faintly. "I believe you."

Phil sank back down into the chair, a big part of his tension gone. "Thanks," he said. He shook his head sadly. "I guess you're about the only one in Seacrest who does. All those people in the lobby believed Warford."

Scotty settled down in his chair. "Of course they believed him," he said easily. "Warford is a professional politician. He's an expert at making an audience believe what he wants them to believe. Besides, this was his show. He staged the whole thing."

"I'll say he did. He had me up there like a dancing bear. He suckered me into making a fool of myself again."

"He certainly did," Scotty said. "Maybe someday you'll learn not to fall into these traps."

"What am I supposed to do?" Phil demanded. "Do you want me to let Warford nail Dad's hide to the wall without even trying to stop him?"

"You haven't helped your father much so far."

"I know," Phil said, dropping his head again. "After tonight, more people than ever will think he's guilty. Even those who didn't believe it before will think I tried to stop that meeting."

"I suppose they will."

"I'm sorry about Bimbo, too," Phil said slowly. "It wasn't even his fight to begin with, but now I've got him in the doghouse, too."

Scotty chuckled. "I don't think you have to waste any

sympathy on Bimbo," he said. "Warford handled that neatly too. He swung Bimbo's mother over to his side by defending her son, and Mrs. Barnes pulls a lot of weight with the women in this town."

Phil thought of Mrs. Flemming and nodded grimly. Warford had used every angle to his own advantage. Phil felt that he had been so thoroughly discredited in the eyes of the town, he would never be believed again. He understood now why his father had been beaten into exhaustion. Even the strongest man could stand up under Warford's assault only so long. He sighed and looked up. "Maybe I've gained something, but I'm sure learning the hard way." He grinned feebly. "At least I've learned to hold my temper. I didn't blow my top tonight."

"You did a good job," Scotty said seriously. "You've come a long way."

"Maybe it was because I couldn't think of anything to say."

"There wasn't anything you could say in a spot like that," Scotty said. "You would have been in the wrong if you had opened your mouth. They had the cards stacked against you."

Phil didn't care to talk about the incident any more. The scene was too vivid in his mind. Just thinking about what had happened made him sick. "What happened in the meeting?" he asked.

"About what you could expect to happen," Scotty said. "Warford answered the questions he could safely answer and parried the ones that would embarrass him. His claque put on a good show, applauding every time he made a point."

"That's the way I had it figured," Phil said glumly. "Did he mention my father?"

"Not by name." Scotty tapped out his pipe and placed it on the desk. "Warford laid the blame for the accident directly on the city engineer's office, though." Scotty stared down at his hands. "He was cute," he went on. "He played heavily on Sanchez's death. He promised a vigorous investigation and said if any graft or criminal negligence could be proved, immediate steps would be taken."

"What does that mean, Scotty?"

Scotty got to his feet. "I'm afraid it means that Warford is thinking about bringing your father to trial."

CHAPTER 8

At home, Phil found a light burning in the living room. When he saw that no one was downstairs, he went up to his father's room, only to find that empty too. Puzzled, he went back to the living room. His father's absence troubled him, for Dad hadn't worked late at the office for some time now and he certainly had no social life. Phil turned on the television set and tried to watch a late movie, but he was unable to concentrate, so he turned it off and paced the floor.

It had been five days since the accident out at the new building, and so many things had happened since that it was a confused jumble in Phil's mind. He sought a thread he could follow through, but each time he felt he had something, it became so tangled with the other threads that it ended up as a woolly ball in his mind.

First there was the accident itself. What had caused that? According to Phil's father, it had been an inferior mix of concrete, substituted for the mix specified. That meant that the contractor, Herman Osterly, had used a cheaper mix and that Mayor Warford had been in on the deal. The mayor's phone message to be relayed to Osterly proved Warford's guilt. Phil had had the proof of that guilt on tape, but some-

one had learned about the tape and had erased it before anyone had heard it.

Mayor Warford had ordered Osterly to destroy any evidence that they worked together, so now any proof of that
agreement was probably gone forever. Phil's first thread
ended right there.

He started back with the accident again. Victor Sanchez's
death had caused such a stir in Seacrest that Mayor Warford
could not ignore the citizens' demand that something be
done about it. He had settled on the variance and had used
this as an excuse, both to clear himself of any blame and to
use the city engineer as the goat. Carl Martinson had been a
stumbling block to Warford's administration for some time.
If he could convince the citizens that the variance had
caused the accident, then the blame would be on Carl Martinson, not Mayor Warford.

Phil picked up the thread that was King Rooster, and this
was the shortest thread of all. King Rooster was someone
Phil and his father knew, yet he was someone who had betrayed them at every turn. King Rooster, not Mayor Warford,
might be the real boss of Seacrest. Twice now Phil had
been on the verge of exposing Warford, and each time Warford had learned of the plan and had turned the tables on
Phil.

Again Phil checked through the list of those who had
known he had the recorded phone message. There were
Samuel Barnes, Mrs. Barnes, Virgil Charters, Melton Flood,
Scotty, his father, and Jon Hansen. Any one of these people
could have known about the plan Phil and Bimbo had made

to try and trap Mayor Warford at the public forum. Someone had tipped the mayor off.

Phil looked at the clock, and when he saw it was midnight, he began to worry about his father again. A terrible thought struck Phil—Mayor Warford might have decided to do away with the city engineer! Warford would have a perfect alibi for tonight—he was on the stage before hundreds of persons. After some thought, Phil discarded this idea. Warford wouldn't be likely to do away with the man he had selected to take the blame. Warford needed Carl Martinson, Phil thought, and felt his father was safe physically, at least for the time being.

Phil went upstairs and climbed into bed. He had intended to lie awake until his father came in, but the events of the day and evening had been too big a strain, and he fell asleep.

It was eight the next morning when Phil walked into the kitchen. Mrs. Flemming was standing at the kitchen sink peeling vegetables for their Sunday dinner. She looked up when Phil came in. "Shh," she said, placing the paring knife to her lips, "your father's still asleep."

Phil nodded. He had awakened at four in the morning, checked, and found his father in bed. "He needs the rest," he said.

Mrs. Flemming nodded vigorously. "He certainly does. He didn't get in until after one o'clock this morning. I don't know what you and your father are coming to."

Phil knew Mrs. Flemming well enough to know she had something important on her mind. "Why me?" he asked, expecting the worst.

"Your father staying out until all hours of the night—and

you getting into trouble with the police." Mrs. Flemming hacked disapprovingly at a carrot.

Phil groaned. "Bad news travels fast," he said.

"I've had three telephone calls—three of them, mind you —already this morning telling me all about it."

"I suppose you told your callers that I was a bad boy and that I was lucky the police didn't throw me in jail."

"I did not," Mrs. Flemming said indignantly. "I told them not to bother me with such foolishness until they knew what they were talking about. I told them I'd known you, boy and young man, and you wouldn't do anything illegal."

Phil went over and put his arm around the housekeeper's waist. "You're a doll, Mrs. Flemming," he said. "A chubby, living doll."

"Now stop that," Mrs. Flemming said, turning pink. "You're flustering me at my work. You go over and get yourself some cereal. You've been up an hour now without a bite to eat. After breakfast, we'll be off to church."

Phil carried the bowl of cereal into the dining room and was eating at the table when his father walked in. Phil greeted him, but his father only nodded and dropped into a chair. As Mrs. Flemming brought in a cup of coffee, Phil studied his father's face. There was no sign of what might have happened the night before, except that his father looked a bit more worn.

While his father sipped his coffee, Phil mulled over whether he should tell him about Mayor Warford's threat to bring charges. It would be better if Dad heard the news here, he decided, instead of having someone outside tell him.

His father looked over the rim of his cup. "How did you do at the meeting last night, son?"

As Phil explained, his father's face grew more drawn and haggard. "They won't do anything more about it," Phil said.

The cup rattled in the saucer when his father tried to set it down. "It was things like this that made me want to keep you out of this mess."

"Don't worry about me. I'm not hurt. It wasn't me personally they were after. It was you."

"I know, son, I know." His father stared at the tablecloth. "But they're attacking you to get at me. Maybe I should give up—get out of the office."

Phil laid his spoon down and leaned forward. "It's too late for that now. They won't let you bow out. Mayor Warford needs a goat to cover up his part in that building accident. He's picked you. Dad, last night he told that audience he was going to push an investigation for graft or criminal negligence against your office."

Mr. Martinson's mouth sagged and his gray face went white. His eyes began to look glazed. "No," he said feebly, "no, he couldn't do that—no."

Phil was shocked as he looked at his father. Carl Martinson had never been a vigorous man, but Phil had always thought of him as being strong. Now that strength all seemed suddenly to have drained away.

Mrs. Flemming entered with a plate of bacon and eggs. She stared as Mr. Martinson tried to wave the food away, his hand trembling violently in the air. Mrs. Flemming backed away, still holding the plate, her eyes round with horror.

"Mr. Martinson," she gasped. "You're sick, real sick. I'll call Dr. Calvin."

Phil jumped up, took the plate of food, and set it on the table before he went over to his father. "Let me help you, Dad. We'll go into the other room, and you can lie down on the divan." He put his head and shoulders under his father's arm and lifted him to his feet. Carl Martinson's body hung limp and helpless against Phil, but with Mrs. Flemming on the other side to steady the load, Phil managed to get his father into the front room and down on the divan. He took off his father's coat and tie before he lowered his head to the pillow Mrs. Flemming had brought. Then he started toward the phone, but stopped when he heard Mrs. Flemming calling Dr. Calvin.

Phil followed the ambulance to the hospital and waited in the reception room for almost two hours before Dr. Calvin came in. "How is he?" Phil asked.

"He's resting," the doctor said. "I know that's a timeworn expression, and it doesn't give much comfort. But in your father's case, that's about all I can say."

"What's wrong with him?"

"I don't know yet, son. Perhaps it's complete mental and physical exhaustion."

"He's been through enough to exhaust an elephant," Phil said grimly. "I suppose you know about that."

"I've heard gossip."

A feeling that approached panic gripped Phil when he realized his father's life might lie in the hands of someone who thought him guilty. Phil grabbed the doctor's arm. "Do you think he did what they're accusing him of?" he demanded hoarsely.

"Son," the doctor said quietly, "to a doctor, the guilt or innocence of a patient has no bearing. If your father and Mayor Warford were lying side by side, each would receive every bit of professional skill I could command."

Phil dropped his hand. "Sure," he said quietly. "I'm sorry; I should have known better than to think a thing like that."

"You're worn out yourself," Dr. Calvin said. "From what I understand, you've been through quite a bit yourself lately."

Phil managed a small grin. "I'm young. I can bounce back."

"Not forever," the doctor said drily. "We'll have to give your father a series of tests before I can come to any definite conclusion. In the meantime, he must have complete rest."

"You think he should stay here?"

"Definitely," the doctor said firmly. "And he needs twenty-four-hour care." He hesitated as he looked at Phil. "I could arrange for nurses, if you want me to."

"Thanks, doctor, I would appreciate it." Phil looked over hopefully. "Is there any chance of my seeing him now?"

The doctor shook his head. "No visitors for the present," he said. "I'll be back around three this afternoon and look in on him again."

"I'll see you this afternoon then, doctor." Phil's throat tightened as he watched Dr. Calvin leave. He thought of his father lying in one of the impersonal rooms, alone and helpless, on a cold white bed.

Mrs. Flemming had gone to church and come back by the time Phil got home. They had a somber dinner, and then he returned to the hospital. Phil jumped up when the doctor entered the reception room. He searched Dr. Calvin's face for some sign of his father's condition. If anything, the doctor seemed more cheerful, Phil thought. "Can I see him?" he asked abruptly.

Dr. Calvin nodded his head slightly. "For five minutes. Your father is a mighty sick man."

"Do you know anything yet?"

"No. As I told you this morning, we'll have to wait for the results of the tests. That may take some time. Remember, five minutes," the doctor said. "Your father is in room 132."

Phil pushed open the door of 132 without knocking. A bright-eyed young nurse rose from a chair and came forward.

"I'm Phil Martinson," Phil said in a low voice. "The doctor said I could see my father."

"I'm Miss King." She moved toward the door and her crisp uniform rustled as she left.

Phil looked over. He saw that his father was conscious, but he wouldn't have known the still figure lying there; it bore little resemblance to the father he had always known. He walked softly to the foot of the bed. "Hello, Dad," he said and tried to grin.

A faint smile touched his father's lips. "Hello, son."

"Dr. Calvin said I could only stay five minutes. You're going to be out of here in no time." Phil looked around the room. "What a cushy setup—a swell place to spend a vacation." He managed to chuckle. "Maybe I'll see if I can't reserve one of these places for a few days myself." He knew his attempt at humor had been feeble, but it was all he could think of to say.

"Son," his father said weakly, "come here."

Phil picked up the chair the nurse had occupied and carried it up near the bed. "Is this better?" he asked when he sat down.

"After you left for the meeting last night, I had a phone call." His father paused and closed his eyes.

"Maybe you shouldn't try to talk. You can tell me next time."

His father made impatient little motions with his hand on the bed cover. "It was a man—he wouldn't tell me his name—he talked with a lisp. He said he had something that would prove I didn't cause that accident."

Phil leaned forward. "He said he had proof?"

"He told me to meet him out at Rock Hill Cemetery in an hour."

"Let me do the talking, Dad. You went out to Rock Hill Cemetery." Phil waited until his father nodded. "And you met this man."

"No, I waited until midnight, but . . ." His father's voice trailed off into nothing. Phil grasped his wrist.

"Don't try to say anything more. Just lie there and rest." Panic gripped Phil as he looked at his father's closed eyes. He felt for the pulse and found it, wavering and weak. "I'll take care of everything, Dad. Don't you worry about it. Things are going to work out fine."

"I'm afraid your five minutes are up."

Phil turned to see Miss King holding the door open.

"Sure," Phil said rising. He realized he still held his father's wrist, and he gave it a squeeze. Miss King still held the door open. "Coming," Phil said and laid his father's hand gently down on the cover.

The next morning Phil told Scotty about his father's illness. Phil had never known the photographer to show emotion, but as he listened, Scotty's eyes were troubled and there was no cynical twist to his lips. Scotty sounded sincere when he expressed his sorrow, and kind when he told Phil not to try to work any regular hours as long as his father was in the hospital.

Later, Bimbo dropped into the studio and Scotty suggested they both leave. At the malt shop, Phil told Bimbo about the phone call his father had received. "I don't know anyone who talks with a lisp," Phil said. "Do you?"

Bimbo shook his head. "I wonder why the guy didn't show up after taking all the trouble to call?"

Phil had wondered this himself. The call could have been a practical joke—or a means to lure his father out to the cemetery for some other purpose. He finally told Bimbo that if the phone call was on the level, then whoever had called must have been working for Mayor Warford.

"What makes you think the guy with the lisp was one of Warford's men?" Bimbo asked.

"If it had been a friend of Dad's, he would have given his name. And this business of meeting out at the cemetery . . . Why would the guy pick a lonesome spot like that unless he wanted to make sure they weren't seen together. Finally, no one but somebody who worked for Warford would be likely to have information that would help Dad."

"Maybe it was King Rooster," Bimbo said.

"But King Rooster has to be somebody we know, and we don't know anyone who talks with a lisp."

"Maybe the lisp was put on," Bimbo said.

"That's possible," Phil agreed. "But this is the only lead we have, and I'm going to follow it up from every angle."

Bimbo looked up quickly. "You're not thinking of going out to the cemetery at night, are you?"

"That's one of the angles. This guy made a date to meet Dad out there at night. Maybe he haunts the place." Phil had been only half-serious about this suggestion, but he had another idea, one he intended to put into action. If the caller actually worked for Warford, then perhaps Jon Hansen would be able to give them a lead. Phil remembered that he had promised his father that he would apologize to the custodian for entering Leppert's office without permission. Now it seemed that he could make one trip to city hall serve two purposes.

CHAPTER 9

Phil had told Bimbo of his plan to visit city hall, and Bimbo had agreed to come over to the Martinson home. Early that evening, Bimbo called and told Phil to pick him up on a side street.

"What's the idea of meeting me here?" Phil demanded when Bimbo climbed into the car.

"My mother says you're a bad influence," Bimbo said blandly. "I'm not supposed to come over to your place anymore."

"Great! How's that supposed to make me feel?"

"It's a distinction," Bimbo said. "Not everybody can be a bad influence, you know."

"OK," Phil said and jammed the car into gear. "Maybe you'd better pull out. I don't want to corrupt your morals."

"Aw, come off it," Bimbo wheedled. "I didn't think you'd get sore. Gosh, it doesn't do any harm to play along like this. It gets me off the hook at home."

Phil didn't answer. He realized that Bimbo was right, but still it hurt to have the people of Seacrest think of him as a bad influence. Actually, he was lucky to have a pal stick with him. Bimbo had taken a lot because of Phil. "Forget it," he said pulling up before the city hall. "Being called a bad influence doesn't bother me any."

Phil had worried some about the reception Jon Hansen would give them, but when they found the old custodian coming out of a broom closet, Hansen put out his hand. "Good evening, Phil," he said, "I heard about your father. It was a terrible thing. I'm sorry, awfully sorry."

"Thank you, Mr. Hansen. I want to apologize for the last time I was here, when I slipped into . . ."

"Quiet," Hansen said sternly. "That is past." He looked up and down the hall cautiously before he came closer. "I told you I wouldn't help you before, but now after what they've done to your father—could I do something for you?"

It gave Phil a warm feeling to know that his father still had one friend in Seacrest. He felt he could now take Jon Hansen into his confidence. He explained about the phone call his father had received from the man with a lisp. "Do you know anybody like that around here?" he asked.

Hansen pushed the khaki cap back on his head. "With a lisp, eh?" he said thoughtfully, then shook his head. "I'm afraid not, son." Suddenly the old man's face lit up. "Wait a minute, I just thought of something. One night a fellow who sometimes works late called me to make sure he had locked a file cabinet. I never noticed that this fellow lisped, until I heard him on the telephone. I guess he held his lips close . . ."

"Who was this man, Mr. Hansen?"

"He's a fellow by the name of Leon Yater. He's a little, skinny fellow, and almost bald. He works up in the accounting department on the second floor." Hansen went on to explain that he had been working back on the first floor all evening and had no idea whether Leon Yater had come in. "Suppose we go up and see," he said.

The old custodian led the way up the stairs and down a hallway. When they stopped before a set of double doors, Phil saw the lights were out inside. "I guess he isn't here," he said.

Hansen went inside and snapped on the light switch. The fluorescent lights flickered, then burst into white brilliance. Hansen took the boys back to a desk in the corner. "This is Leon Yater's desk," he said.

Phil saw that the top of the desk didn't even have a mail basket on it. The chair was pushed in close. "Have the cleaning women been in here yet?" he asked.

"No," Hansen said. "They won't be here for an hour."

Phil pointed to the empty wastepaper basket beside the desk. "It looks as though Yater didn't work today."

Bimbo peered into the empty basket. "Maybe the guy's neat," he said.

"No one can work all day without throwing away at least one scrap of paper," Phil said. "Either this basket has been emptied, or Yater wasn't here today."

Hansen scratched his head. "Come to think of it, I haven't seen the fellow around here in some time. Course I only work nights," he said apologetically. He nodded when Phil reached down and took hold of a drawer handle. "Go ahead," he said heartily, "search anything you want. I'm behind you and your pa."

There was nothing in the top drawer but clean scratch pads and forms that had not been filled in. The other drawers yielded nothing more. There wasn't a scratch of writing in the desk. "Looks as if this desk has been cleaned out," Phil said.

Bimbo nodded soberly. "Maybe he took off."

"If he did, he forgot his eyeshade." Phil lifted the shade from a nail at the side of the desk.

"He always wore that when he worked," Hansen explained. "Makes him look right comical, with those few stray red hairs stretched across that bald head."

"You said he's small and skinny?"

"I'll bet that man doesn't weigh much more than a hundred pounds," Hansen said. "He's a quiet little cuss. Grouchy too—never a 'good evening' for anybody. Leon Yater isn't a fellow you'd cotton up to much."

Phil felt that they'd found all the office had to offer, so the three of them returned to the first floor, where Phil thanked the old man for his help. Hansen again promised any aid he could give, and Phil promised to convey Hansen's good wishes to his father on his next visit to the hospital. "You don't know where this Leon Yater lives, do you?" Phil asked.

"Nope, don't have the least idea. You'd have to get that in the personnel department in the daytime."

Phil went over what they had learned on the way back to the car. It wasn't much, but they did know the man's name and they had a description—if he was the man who had phoned. "Bimbo," Phil said as they drove off, "you're going down to city hall tomorrow and try to find out where this Yater lives. I'm poison down there."

"Sure," Bimbo said, yawning. "As long as I'm really a pure boy at heart, they may think I'm worth saving."

Scotty was not in the studio when Phil arrived the next morning. Phil had done some deep thinking the night before and had come to some definite conclusions. He liked his job here at the studio, but he felt his presence could be harmful to Scotty's business. Feeling against Carl Martinson was running high in town, and since the episode in the lobby of the civic auditorium, Phil himself was generally regarded in a bad light.

There were people in Seacrest who would hesitate to call Scotty for party or wedding pictures if they thought Phil Martinson would be sent out to shoot the job.

When Scotty came in a few minutes later, Phil told him of his decision. Scotty walked over and picked up some papers. "When I don't want you around here anymore, I'll fire you," he said.

Phil continued to argue, then settled on a compromise. "Suppose I do stay," he said, "and only work in the darkroom."

"If that's the way you want it," Scotty replied gruffly.

Phil called Dr. Calvin's office as soon as he thought the doctor would be in. No, there was nothing new to report on his father's condition, he was told. The results of the tests were not in, and Dr. Calvin didn't yet know when they would be available. There were to be no more visits, the doctor told Phil, until he was notified otherwise.

Phil wanted to protest, but he realized Dr. Calvin was doing this for his father's own good. He thanked the doctor and promised to call again the next day.

Phil found he could do more constructive thinking when he kept busy, so he spent the rest of the morning developing and printing a batch of pictures. It was three in the afternoon, and Phil was putting new labels on the chemical bottles, when Bimbo walked in. He held out an open paper bag. "Have a cookie," he said. "I stopped by a bakery."

Phil reached in. "I hope the bakery was on the way over here from the city hall."

"It was," Bimbo said cheerfully. "But I might as well have stayed away from that place. They wouldn't tell me a thing in personnel. I turned on all my charm, but still no soap. I went up to the office where we were last night, but Yater's desk was empty. They said he wasn't in, and they didn't know when he'd be back. Everybody seemed to clam up when I mentioned Yater's name."

"That's tough," Phil said, and he knew the disappointment showed in his voice.

Bimbo popped another cookie into his mouth. "But old bloodhound Barnes stayed on the job," he said. "I hung around until the coffee break and talked to a woman who belongs to Mother's club. She works in that office. She doesn't know Leon Yater; she said nobody there knows him very well. She said this Yater does personal work for Warford and Leppert, and he doesn't have much to do with any of the rest of the office staff."

"Works for Warford and Leppert, eh?" Phil said thoughtfully. "That would give him a chance to handle some confidential material."

"That's what I figured. This woman said Yater hadn't been to work since last Wednesday."

"Wednesday?" Phil said. "Let's see, that would be a week,

tomorrow. This fellow with the lisp called Dad last Saturday night. Did she tell you anything more about Yater?"

"She knew he drives an old car, but she didn't have any idea where he lives." Bimbo peered into the bag to count the remaining cookies. "Here, have another," he said.

Phil posted on the last label and then washed his hands. "That last cookie tasted like hypo," he said. "Let me try another."

Bimbo's mouth was full. "Too late," he said in a muffled voice as he wadded up the bag and tossed it into the wastepaper basket. "Besides, Mrs. Flemming would give you the devil for spoiling your appetite."

Since early that morning, Phil had tried to work out a definite plan of action. None of the ideas, except one, had seemed to offer much. This one idea centered around the place the caller had chosen to meet Phil's father. Rock Hill was the old cemetery that stood on the edge of town. There had been little new building in that direction, so there were only a few houses around the place.

He decided to try his idea out on Bimbo. "Why do you suppose that guy told my father to meet him at Rock Hill Cemetery?"

"So they could be alone, I guess."

"But Rock Hill is a lonely place," Phil said. "Anyone going out there might look suspicious."

"Then it was because the guy lived near Rock Hill."

Phil snapped his fingers. "That's what I hoped you'd say. I think we should drive out there and look around."

"Before dark," Bimbo said quickly.

"Right now," Phil said. "I'm through in here, and Scotty will let me off."

Phil drove down the two lane asphalt road that ran beside the cemetery wall. There was an archway in the center of the wall, but the other three sides of the cemetery were enclosed by a chain-link fence. This was still a part of the town, and the few streets there were had names, but the houses were few and far between. Phil pulled off on the dirt shoulder across from the archway and stopped.

"What now?" Bimbo asked.

"I want to get the lay of the land."

"Why don't you ask some of the inhabitants in there?" Bimbo said, pointing to the arch. "Some of them have been around here for a long time."

"Very funny. You're no help."

A car came from the direction of town and passed them. It continued on and turned up a private road that led to the first house beyond the cemetery. "Looks as if they have live inhabitants around here, too," Bimbo said.

Phil started the motor. "I think I'll take your suggestion and have a talk with them."

Phil stopped in the drive beside the house, and almost immediately a large Irish setter dashed around the corner, barking furiously. "Down, Red!" a voice called. "Down!" A man appeared from behind the house and took the dog by the collar. "He isn't vicious," the man said, "just noisy."

Phil climbed out, while Bimbo stayed in the car eyeing the dog. "My name is Phil Martinson." Phil hoped the name wouldn't mean anything. "We're looking for a man we think might live around here. His name is Leon Yater."

The man frowned as he scratched Red behind the ears. "Yater?" he said thoughtfully. "Sounds familiar, but I don't think I know him. Are you sure he lives around here?"

The question stopped Phil. He didn't know how he could explain why they thought Leon Yater lived around Rock Hill Cemetery. "He's a small, thin man," he finally said. The dog, now free, came over and nuzzled Phil's hand.

"That's not much of a description," the man said.

Bimbo stuck his head out of the car window. "We were told he was seen around here at night," he said.

The man grinned slightly. "Small and thin, eh? Yater? Of course! That was the name of our ghost."

"Ghost?" Bimbo said.

"That's what my wife and I call him. I don't know the man, but I'd seen him a few times at night when I took Red out for a walk. I'd see him down by the cemetery, but before I could speak to him, he'd disappear."

"Disappear?" Bimbo said.

"He didn't really disappear. I don't believe in those things, myself. This fellow would duck into the brush beside the road. About a week ago, Red ran on ahead of me, and I guess he surprised the man. Anyway, when I got up there, Red was sniffing at a coat on the ground."

"Was there any identification in the coat?" Phil asked.

"Yes. This fellow had evidently stopped at his mail box, because there was a piece of bulk mail advertising in the pocket. It was addressed to Leon Yater and it had his street name and number. I felt pretty bad about Red having scared the fellow, so the next morning I took the coat to the address."

Phil was beginning to feel elated. "Did you talk to him?" he asked eagerly.

The man shook his head. "There was nobody home, so I left the coat on the porch with a note of apology."

Phil reached down and patted Red. "Good dog," he said. When the man had given them the address, the boys thanked him and drove away.

They found the house on the other side of the cemetery. Almost all of the homes in the vicinity were modest, but this house was little more than a shack. The frame building was set far back from the road. There was no driveway, but twin lines of flattened weeds showed where a car had been driven up to the empty garage.

Phil parked the car beside the house and the boys climbed up on the porch. "I don't think we'll find anybody home," Phil said. He noticed that the door stood open a crack, and he rapped on the jamb. He waited and knocked again. When there was no answer, he stepped back and Bimbo took his place. Bimbo gave the door a resounding whack with the palm of his hand. "Hey, what are you doing?" Phil said.

Bimbo grinned as the door swung open. He stuck his head in. "Wow!" he yelled as he pulled back out. "Take a look in there."

Phil looked in. The front room was a shambles. A table lay on its side, with an overturned lamp nearby. One of the window curtains hung by one corner. "It looks as though there was a brawl in here," he said.

Bimbo started back off the porch. "We'd better call the police," he said.

"I thought you'd had enough of the Seacrest police," Phil

said. "Call them and we'll end up in jail for causing all this damage." He poked his head in the door. "Is there anyone in there?" he called.

In the silence that followed, Bimbo trailed Phil into the front room. "Gosh, what a mess," he said looking around.

The boys made a quick tour of the house. It didn't take long, for there were only three rooms and a bath; but each room had been torn apart. Dresser drawers lay on the floor in the bedroom, and pots and pans were strewn around in the kitchen. "Where do you suppose the body is?" Bimbo said when they were in the front room again.

"I don't think there is a body." Phil looked around the room. "Do you notice anything funny?"

"I don't dig your sense of humor," Bimbo said. "You think this is funny?"

Phil ignored Bimbo's remark. "There was a search made here, but I'm sure it was made after Leon Yater had left."

"Did you find a farewell note?"

"Cut it out." Phil walked into the bedroom and opened the closet door. "Look in there," he said. "No clothes, not even a pair of shoes."

"Maybe Yater didn't own any clothes except the stuff he wore."

"He'd at least have a spare shirt and extra socks." Phil pointed down at the empty dresser drawers.

"Maybe whoever did away with him took his clothes with them."

"That doesn't make sense to me. I can't see someone wrecking a place and then stopping to pack clothes before they left. Look, there isn't even a toothbrush or a razor in the bathroom. No, this was a crude job. Whoever did it was only interested in trying to find something."

"They must have made a lot of noise," Bimbo said. "I guess they didn't care who heard them."

Phil paced the floor, trying to construct a pattern. There had been a search made here, but for what? The search hadn't been localized—it had been spread through every room. Even the floorboards had been pried up under the laundry sink on the service porch. He walked back into the front room and kicked a pillow. The cover had been slit and the stuffing leaked out.

"Do you suppose they found what they were after?" Bimbo asked.

"Who knows?"

"Let's get out of here," Bimbo said, starting for the front door. "This place is beginning to give me the creeps." He walked out in the yard and waited while Phil stood on the porch. "What are you waiting for now?" he asked.

Phil was trying to decide what to do next. He had given his name to the man at the other house, and once the damage was discovered, the man would remember sending the boys over here. Phil considered going back and reporting that there had been nobody home. He realized this wouldn't furnish a solid alibi. He sighed, closed the front door, and decided the best he and Bimbo could do was to hope the mystery of Leon Yater's disappearance would be cleared up before the wreckage was discovered.

CHAPTER 10

$\mathbf{P}_{\text{HIL}}$ DROPPED Bimbo off and then drove home. He opened the front door to find a sober-faced Mrs. Flemming waiting for him in the front hallway. "A porter from the city hall brought a box this afternoon," she said and pointed to the front room. "I put it in there."

The lettering on the cardboard carton said it had contained scouring powder. A heavy cord held it closed. Phil walked to the table and untied the knot, then pulled up the cardboard flaps. He reached in and took out a memorandum pad. "Why, this is Dad's stuff," he said.

Mrs. Flemming nodded miserably. "The porter said they had ordered him to clean out Mr. Martinson's desk and bring it all over here. That's all there was."

Slowly Phil took the items out, piece by piece. There were a desk pen set, a pack of blotters, a few technical manuals, an address book, some rubber stamps, and a small box that contained other office supplies. Phil laid them all on the table. "They pounced on Dad like a flock of vultures," he said bitterly.

Mrs. Flemming's eyes were filled with tears. "The porter said he was sorry," she sobbed.

Phil went over and dropped into his father's easy chair.

He stared at the articles on the table. "Not much to show for twelve years of hard work and heartbreak, is it?" He blinked and gulped hard. "Is dinner ready?" he asked and stood up.

The next morning, Phil told Scotty how they had sent his father's belongings home. Scotty tapped his fingers on the desk. "If your father had anything in the office that was going to help him, it's gone now," he said.

Phil had thought of that. He realized that Dad's desk and files had doubtless been rifled, and any evidence to prove he was innocent had been destroyed. "Dad was too trusting," he said. "He wouldn't believe anyone was dishonest until they proved it."

Phil felt restless, and because there was no darkroom work that was pressing, he explained a plan he had worked out the night before. "I think I'll stay on the road out there in front of that building and take some pictures," he told Scotty. "They won't let me near the building, but if I use that 200mm telephoto lens, I should be able to get some close-up shots. Maybe there'll be something that will help Dad."

"I don't know what you hope to get," Scotty said cynically. "If they've already put the new wall up . . ."

"Anything is better than sitting around doing nothing," Phil said irritably. "I feel guilty about every minute I waste."

"If you feel that way, go ahead."

Phil got out his own 35mm single lens reflex camera and the telephoto lens. The lens was in its own carrying case, so Phil put this into his pocket. He would mount it on the camera once he was ready to shoot the pictures, for the camera was awkward to handle when it was on.

Traffic was light at this time of the morning on Ramona Road. Things would begin to liven up when the honky-tonks and cheap joints opened up in the afternoon, but now there was little on the road but delivery trucks. Phil let traffic set his pace and stayed well behind a heavy sedan that traveled sedately ahead of him. His thoughts were on Leon Yater and what might have happened to the little man, so he scarcely noticed when the heavy sedan suddenly pulled up to run abreast of another car. He stared when instead of passing, the sedan moved in, forcing the other car over. "What's the crazy fool doing?" Phil muttered.

When they were in front of a driveway that led to a parking space, the sedan veered over sharply, and with a screech of tires and brakes, both cars swung into the parking area and stopped.

Phil braked his own car over to the side of the road. He had hit the ground and was running before he realized he had the camera in his hand. The stalled cars were still over a hundred feet ahead when he unsnapped the case. Phil had no idea what was going on, but he knew he wanted to get it on film.

Two men had leaped from the heavy sedan and were dragging a third man from the other car. Phil glanced down to make the diaphragm setting and check the shutter speed as he ran. When he reached the parking area, the two men had pulled their struggling victim to the corner of the building. Phil saw that they would disappear in a moment, so he dropped to one knee, twisting the focusing knob to infinity.

The men saw Phil, and one of them broke away and charged. Phil saw the man coming. He changed the focus, and waited until the last split second before he snapped the shutter and threw himself to one side. A shoe caught Phil in the thigh as the man passed, and Phil curled his body around the camera, waiting for the man to return and kick him again.

When there was no assault, Phil looked up. He scrambled to his feet and, as he saw the men running for their car, pulled the film advance lever around to take another shot. He had his second picture when the heavy sedan swung around in a shower of gravel and bore down on him. There was a light standard six feet away, and with a wild leap and a dive, Phil made it behind the base as the car rushed by.

He got to his knees and watched it sway violently as it turned into Ramona Road and sped away. Brushing off dirt and gravel, he walked back to the building, where the third man stood. Phil looked up with a start. "Mr. Charters!" he said.

The short, chubby man was trembling. His lips were blue, and his hand shook as he pulled a handkerchief from his pocket and wiped his face. "Those hoodlums," he said through chattering teeth. He stopped and looked at Phil. "Why, it's the Martinson boy."

"Yes, sir, Mr. Charters. Are you hurt?"

"No, I don't think so." The man was regaining his composure fast now that he realized he was safe. He looked at the camera in Phil's hand. "I say, that thing is better than a gun to scare off crooks."

"Maybe so, but it isn't much protection." Phil rubbed his thigh where the man had kicked him. He looked back at the road. No one had stopped. The action had been swift, and the attack had taken place in the parking area, so it had gone unnoticed. They stood in front of a place called *The Diggings*, and a card in the door read *Closed*.

"It's getting so an honest citizen isn't safe here anymore," Charters said on the way back to his car. "Not even in broad daylight." The man looked embarrassed as he stood beside his car. "I certainly owe you something for what you did, young man." He started to pull his wallet out.

"You don't owe me anything," Phil said quickly. "Not any money." Phil hesitated as Charters stood, with the wallet still in his hand. Phil thought he should tell Charters that what he really wanted was understanding. He wanted Charters to listen while he explained about his father. He wanted the man's help, but the words wouldn't come out. Anything Charters might do now would be because he was under obligation to Phil, not because he believed Carl Martinson was innocent. "I don't want a reward," he said curtly.

Charters replaced his wallet and slid in behind the wheel of his car. "I certainly want to thank you, young man. You saved me quite a sum of money."

Phil hadn't stopped to think why the men had forced Charters in here. "Were they going to rob you?" he asked.

Charters stared at Phil. "Of course," he said. "I often carry large sums of money to close some of my deals." He slammed the car door and started the motor.

Phil turned and limped back to his own car. He was half-angry at himself for not making Virgil Charters listen to him when he had the chance. Perhaps it had been stupid pride that had kept him from forcing the issue. Phil snorted. "I guess I've got too much of Dad in me," he said and grinned to himself.

Phil gave up the idea of taking pictures of the building, for the day at least. Instead, he returned to town and stopped in at Dr. Calvin's office.

Half an hour later the nurse motioned to him, and when she called his name, Phil saw some of the patients in the room look up sharply. He straightened his shoulders and walked into the inner office.

Dr. Calvin rose, shook hands, and indicated a chair beside his desk. "I'm glad you dropped in," he said.

"If it's about your bill . . ." Phil began.

The doctor waved this away. "I want to talk to you about your father. The results from the tests seem to indicate there is really nothing organically wrong with him."

"Do your tests show when a man's heart is broken?"

Dr. Calvin picked up a pencil and rolled it between his thumb and fingers. "No, I don't suppose they would."

Phil's jaw muscles tightened. "That's why my father's lying in the hospital, doctor, and some of the good citizens of Seacrest put him there. Mayor Warford was the instrument, but it was really the people of this town who whipped Dad. One by one, those he thought were friends deserted him, and each time a little of him died."

"Aren't you being a bit harsh on these people? Do they know your father's side of the story? Have they ever been told?"

"I guess not," Phil said slowly. He remembered how even he hadn't known about his father's struggle until a little over a week ago. "Dad doesn't know how to defend himself when he knows he isn't guilty. When I told him last Sunday that Mayor Warford had said he was going to bring charges against him, that was the last straw."

"This answers something that has been troubling me," Dr. Calvin said. "Almost all people want to live, son. But if that desire to live isn't there . . ." Dr. Calvin dropped the pencil and spread his hands.

Phil leaned forward. "You mean my father is going to die?"

"I didn't say that. But if we could restore his will to live, it would be much easier. At least it would do him a great deal more good than any medication I could prescribe."

"If you'd let me talk to him, maybe I could convince him things are going to be all right."

The doctor studied Phil. "Do you think they're going to be all right?" he asked.

"I—I don't know."

"You'd never convince him. It's taken him a long time to reach this state, and mere words aren't going to restore his faith."

Phil studied the top of the desk. "You mean the only way is to have the people of Seacrest believe that he's really innocent."

"I'm afraid that's the only thing. I wish I could help, but I'm not a politician or an orator. I'm a physician, and my powers are limited."

Phil rose and shook hands. "Thank you, doctor. I'm going to prove that Dad is innocent, somehow."

"I wouldn't wait too long," Dr. Calvin said quietly.

When Phil entered the photo studio, he found Bimbo alone in the office. Bimbo was slumped down in a chair, his chin resting on his breastbone. "Scotty was called out," he said. "I told him I'd answer the phone."

Phil saw that something was troubling Bimbo. "What's eating you, pal?" he asked.

"Mother says I have to go down to Los Angeles next week to get things lined up for college in the fall."

Phil knew that two weeks ago this would have been the biggest news in his life; now it seemed insignificant. Even the thought that he wouldn't be going didn't bother him. He felt no great pang when he thought he would never be able to go to college now. None of that seemed important compared to his father's life. "You're getting a big break and don't realize it," he told Bimbo.

"I don't want to go to school if you're not going," Bimbo muttered.

"Well, I can't go, and that's that. Now snap out of it and stop acting like a kid." Phil thought how much his words sounded like Scotty's advice to him. Bimbo cheered up some when Phil told him about Virgil Charters' being nearly hijacked.

Bimbo stayed with Phil while he developed the short strip of film. The film size was so small that it was impossible to tell much from the negative, so Phil made a print while the negative was still wet. He snapped on the lights and took the eight by ten print from the hypo.

"Gosh," Bimbo said, "that guy was right on top of you. Too bad he had his arm up like that so you can't see his face."

"I couldn't wait until he brought it down," Phil said. He dropped the photo back into the tank and printed up his second shot. It showed the two men running to the car. Their backs were turned, so this picture was no good for identification either. "Those pictures may sell," Phil said, striving to keep the pride out of his voice.

"I wish I'd been along," Bimbo said. "You have all the luck."

Phil was thoughtful as they walked back into the office. "Virgil Charters is a friend of your family, isn't he?"

"My folks know him. They've known him a long time, I guess. He's with my dad in the Citizens' Protective League."

"What kind of a fellow is Charters?"

"He's a guy. I don't know. I never thought much about him."

"I mean is he a good businessman? Does your father respect him?"

"I guess so," Bimbo said. "My father says Charters knows the value of a dollar, and how to hang on to it—hey, why all these questions about Virgil Charters, anyway?"

Phil grinned. "We probably could have had him as a partner today."

CHAPTER 11

PHIL had the two prints washed, dried, and laid face up on the desk when Scotty came in. Scotty picked them up and looked at each critically while Phil waited. "Good prints," Scotty said. "Keep it up, you'll make a photographer yet." He dropped them back on the desk and picked up the morning mail.

Phil looked over. Bimbo was staring at Scotty with his mouth open.

"Thanks," Phil said, "thanks for the compliment."

"I meant it," Scotty said, studying a circular he had taken from an envelope. "They're all right."

"Come on, Bimbo," Phil said, "let's go over to the malt shop."

Scotty glanced over from the corner of his eye, then chuckled. Phil had been pretty sure Scotty had been giving him the rib, but he was never too sure about the photographer. Scotty dropped the circular and picked up the prints again. "All right, tell me what happened. How did you get these?"

Phil was reluctant at first, but then told how he had made the pictures. "Do you think they might sell?" he asked cautiously.

"They could," Scotty said and pulled his old typewriter out. "Give me the story again," he said rolling in a piece of paper. "Too bad we can't identify the men. That would make them better pictures." He began to type.

Scotty was still typing out the caption when the phone rang. He reached over and answered it, then handed the telephone to Phil. "It's for you," he said.

Phil held his breath for a moment. It could be bad news from the hospital. He closed his eyes and forced himself to answer the call. "Hello there," a warm voice said. "This is Virgil Charters."

Phil's relief was so great that he couldn't answer. He put his hand over the mouthpiece. "It's Mr. Charters," he said.

"Give Virgil my regards," Scotty said without looking up.

Phil spoke into the phone. Charters asked if Phil would come over to the office in the old mill, and make it as soon as possible. "I'll be over right away," Phil said and hung up. He realized he was still weak from the scare he had received when he thought the call was about his father. "Mr. Charters wants me to come over to his office," he said.

"Maybe he wants to give you a reward," Bimbo said.

Phil hadn't mentioned that Charters had offered to pay him that morning. "I don't want a reward. I'm satisfied with the pictures." Charters' call had lifted Phil's spirits more than he let them know. This morning he hadn't asked the man for his help, but since his talk with Dr. Calvin, Phil was desperate. He was going to get Virgil Charters' help, even if he had to demand that help. "I'm sorry," he said to Bimbo, "I'm afraid I'll have to go alone."

"Sure, I get it. This is by invitation only."

Phil had asked questions lately about the old Charters' Feed and Grain Company. He had found that at one time it had employed as many as forty men and had ten trucks on the road. The mill had sold poultry feed to a wide area, but then the farmers had formed co-ops and had established their own feed mills. The finishing blow that had closed the mill altogether had come when the housing developments took over the nearby poultry ranches.

Charters still kept his office in one corner on the first floor of the mill. The rest of the big, barnlike structure was empty except for the machinery that Charters had never been able to sell. The building itself was on a spur railroad track and had fallen into disrepair in the ten years it had stood empty. It had never been repainted, and the outside was a blotched yellow color.

The office was dingy and messy. The first thing Phil noticed when he entered were the stacks of magazines and trade journals against the wall. There were shelves filled with old ledgers, and a big iron safe in the corner. A fly-specked old clock, with the pendulum at rest, hung on the wall over a roll-top desk. Virgil Charters swung around in a swivel chair and beamed at Phil. "Happy you could come over, son," he said heartily. "Have a chair."

"Thank you, Mr. Charters." Phil picked up a straight chair and carried it over to the desk.

"Better dust it off first. Things are rather run-down around here," Charters said. "I don't spend much time here. I do most of my business in the other fellow's office."

"Yes, sir." Phil sat down. This was his first chance really to study Virgil Charters. When the man beamed, his face seemed to light up; only his eyes remained solemn. The eyes were blue, and what hair he had left was mostly gray. Charters used his hands a great deal to punctuate his remarks.

When Charters leaned back, the tilt of the swivel chair lifted his feet off the floor. He regarded Phil solemnly. "I've done quite a bit of thinking since our little incident this morning," he said slowly.

Phil was glad the talk was going to center around what had happened out on Ramona Road. He decided to let Charters do the talking. "Yes, sir," he said.

"I know you refused a cash reward for what you did, so I won't insult you by making that offer again." Charters pressed his chubby fingers together and studied them intently. "And I know you're concerned about your father's welfare."

Phil leaned forward in his chair. "I'm very concerned, Mr. Charters."

"Of course." Charters took his eyes from his fingers and studied the clock on the wall. "I think I may be able to help you along that line," he said slowly.

Phil's fingernails bit into his palms. "I'd be very interested in knowing what it is. I'd appreciate anything you could do that would help my father." When Charters continued to study the clock in silence, Phil held his breath. He didn't want to press too hard; any offer of help should come direct from Charters himself.

Without taking his eyes from the clock, Charters continued, "Last week a stranger came to me with a very peculiar proposition," he said. "This stranger had been working down at city hall for Mayor Warford and, for reasons of his own, had decided to leave. When he left, he took with him certain confidential material that could be most detrimental to the administration."

Phil felt his pulse pound. He was sure Charters was talking about Leon Yater. But again he had to let Charters take the lead. "I see," he said.

"This man came to me because of my connection with the Citizens' Protective League. It seems that after he took this material, he became badly frightened."

"You mean he was afraid of what Warford would do to him?" Phil asked.

Charters pursed his lips. "The man was afraid Warford was going to kill him," he said in a flat tone.

Phil felt he should put an end to this cat and mouse game. If Virgil Charters was going to help him, Charters had the right to know the information Phil had. "I guess the man you are talking about is Leon Yater," he said.

The swivel chair came down with a bump. Charters' blue eyes were round as he stared at Phil. "You know about this?" he demanded.

"No, not all of it, Mr. Charters." Quickly Phil explained that he knew Yater had been an accountant for the mayor and had disappeared. He told how he and Bimbo had found Yater's home ransacked.

Charters nodded. "That search was evidently made by Warford's men when the material was discovered missing. It seems the man had a right to be frightened."

"This material Yater took with him was records, wasn't it? I mean records of Warford's transactions?"

"Yes, and that's how it might affect your father. I understand some of those records contain information about the building that collapsed."

Phil could hardly contain himself. "You mean Yater kept a secret set of books for Mayor Warford?"

Charters smiled faintly. He leaned back again. "Yes, Yater told me he had a complete record of all the moneys paid out and received in secret transactions."

Phil forced himself to think this out rationally. It was wonderful to find that there were records in existence, but they wouldn't do him any good until they were in his hands. "Where is Leon Yater now?" he asked.

"As I told you, Yater was frightened," Charters said, evading a direct answer to Phil's question. "He wanted me to provide asylum for him until he could turn the records over to the proper authorities. As a man interested in cleaning up the city government of Seacrest, I agreed to hide Yater."

Phil thought about the call his father had received. "Tell me, Mr. Charters, did you hide Yater after Saturday night?"

"Yes, it was Sunday." Charters looked puzzled. "Why?"

Phil explained about the phone call.

"I didn't know he had called your father," Charters said. "Yater came here Sunday evening. We hid his old car back there in the mill, and I took him to a place I knew along the coast to hide for a few days."

"Do you have those records now, Mr. Charters?"

Charters shook his head. "No. Although I wanted to put them in a safe place, Yater refused to give them up."

Phil could understand the man's point of view. As long as he held on to the records, he had something to bargain with. "Will you tell me where Mr. Yater is now?"

Charters beamed at Phil again. "That's why I called you over here, son. I'm not only going to tell you where he is—I want you to go out there and see him." Charters went on to tell how he had known a cave along a deserted stretch of beach and how he had taken Leon Yater there. The man needed more supplies, and Charters wanted Phil to take them out tonight.

Phil was happy at the thought of meeting Yater, but in the last week he had learned to be cautious. "You're sending me out there as a reward for helping you this morning?" he asked.

"Not entirely. After thinking over what happened this morning, I'm not so sure it was a case of simple robbery. Warford may have heard a rumor that I either had hidden Yater or knew something about him. I'm convinced now that those men meant to kidnap me and force me to tell where Yater is hiding. I think I'm being shadowed, and I don't want to take a chance on leading Warford's men out to the cave."

Phil thought back over the times Warford had learned his own plans. He wondered who Charters had told about Yater and whether one of them could be King Rooster. He was also concerned about how Charters intended to use those records once he had his hands on them. "Have you told the Citizens' Protective League about the records?" he asked.

"No, I haven't," Charters said. "At one time I would have gone to them right away. Now, things are different. Warford seems to have a pipeline directly into the organization. Of course I'm sure of the old guard, but some of the newer members . . ."

"Like Melton Flood?" Phil asked.

"As long as I haven't any proof, I'd rather not mention names," Charters said, frowning. He smiled again. "Here, I'll draw you a map so you can find that cave." He sketched out a round drawing, and Phil recognized it as a stretch of beach only a few miles from Seacrest. "The cave is right there," Charters said, making an X on the paper. He stood up and rubbed his hands together. "Now if you'll drive around to the side of the building, we'll load the supplies into your car."

Phil found a loading dock on the side of the building, and as he drew up, a large set of double doors was pushed open from the inside and Charters motioned for him to drive in. Phil got out and looked around while Charters pulled the doors closed. He was in a large room, where the only light was filtered in through a few dirty windows. The rest had been boarded up on the outside. This place had evidently been used for loading and servicing trucks. A work bench with a large steel oil drum stood against the wall.

In the far corner was a heap of cardboard cartons, and by the work bench, a pile of grain bags. Against the wall near the double doors, where Phil had entered, stood a wooden platform with a door behind it.

Charters walked over to the grain bags and pulled out one, half-filled with supplies. Phil carried it back to his car and knew the sack contained canned goods from the way it clanked against his leg. He loaded the supplies into the trunk and turned for instructions.

Charters handed him a folded piece of paper. "I wrote a

note," he said. "It tells Yater that you can be trusted and that he is to turn the records over to you."

"What if he won't turn them over?"

"Search the cave," Charters said grimly. "We want those records, and we can't afford to play games until Yater decides to give them up."

Phil agreed with Charters' thinking. Time was important. Dr. Calvin had warned him of that. Besides, Yater might get frightened and disappear. Or what if Warford's men got to him first? If any of those things happened, the records would be lost forever. Phil told himself the only safe way was to have the records in their possession. "If Yater has those records, I'll bring them back," he promised Charters.

Phil fought down his elation as he drove back to the studio. This was the first real, solid break he'd had since he had started. This trip tonight could mean that by tomorrow morning he would have written proof of his father's innocence.

It bothered Phil some that he hadn't mentioned Bimbo to Charters. He realized why he hadn't; he had been afraid Charters would veto the idea of bringing another person in on the deal. But Charters didn't understand Bimbo the way Phil did. Bimbo was loyal to the core. He had worked hard, and Phil had no idea of cutting his friend out now that the end seemed so close.

Phil didn't intend to tell Scotty anything. Scotty had been only lukewarm to Phil's efforts in the past. Phil could understand why his boss couldn't openly help him in his fight against the administration. Scotty was a small businessman, and his existence depended on making no enemies. Samuel

Barnes and Virgil Charters were big enough to fight, but the administration could smash Scotty like a bug if he gave them any trouble.

Bimbo and Scotty were still in the office when Phil returned. Scotty was sealing up a large manila envelope with Phil's prints inside. He didn't look at Phil.

"Did Charters give you a reward?" Bimbo asked eagerly.

"He offered me a reward," Phil said, careful not to mention when the offer had been made. He hoped Bimbo wouldn't ask any more questions in front of Scotty. "I didn't deserve a reward," he went on. "I was trying to get a good news shot, and I got one. I'm satisfied. I didn't try to save Charters. I didn't even know who he was until after those guys drove away."

"Charters didn't have to know you didn't do it for him," Bimbo said peevishly.

Scotty picked up the envelope and walked to the door. "I'm going down to the post office and mail this in," he said. "I don't know when I'll get back."

Bimbo waited until the door had closed. "Gosh," he exploded, "you'd think he'd want to stay and hear what happened over at Charters' office."

"He didn't want to know, you goof. That was his way of letting us talk in private."

"The guy must have ice water in his veins. I couldn't stand it."

Phil sighed elaborately. "All right, nosey, here's what happened." He told Bimbo how Leon Yater had come to Charters for help, and about the records.

"No wonder the guy was scared," Bimbo said. "If some-body tore up my house like that, I'd take off, too."

"Yater probably took off before the house was searched. He might have been hiding out in a room or somewhere from Wednesday, when he disappeared, to Sunday, when Charters took him out to the cave."

"Cave?"

Phil went on to explain how Yater was hiding in the cave and how they were going out there with the supplies. He pulled out the map Charters had drawn and smoothed it down on the desk. "I hope we can find it in the dark," he said.

The boys studied the map while Phil explained where the section of beach was located. "Hey, I know that cave," Bimbo said. "A couple of years ago the family went there on a beach party. Charters was along, and he and I climbed up to explore that cave. He must have remembered it and figured it was a good place to hide out." Bimbo nodded em-phatically. "I could lead you there blindfolded."

"Good, then it's settled. We'll go out after dark. Where'll we meet?"

"At your place," Bimbo said easily. "Nobody'll see me leave home—my folks are going out to dinner tonight."

There were cold cuts on the table when Phil arrived home that evening. Mrs. Flemming made little pretense of cooking these days. Phil's hours had been irregular, and he ate little when he did come home. He never noticed what they had for dinner.

After she had said grace, Mrs. Flemming looked up. "You

haven't been seeing much of anybody but Bimbo lately, it seems. Haven't you made any plans for the weekend?"

"No," Phil answered wearily, thinking that Bimbo himself had suggested that they take Barbara and Ann to a movie on Friday night with some others of the gang, and he had turned down the idea at once.

"For goodness sakes, why don't you?" Mrs. Flemming said indignantly. "You can't stay here, holed up like a hermit. It would do you good to get out with the other young folks. I know Mr. Martinson would want you to go."

Phil knew that this was true, and after dinner he went into the living room and dropped into the easy chair. Was he unwilling to go out for reasons that he wouldn't admit, even to himself? He didn't know how Ann would feel about being seen with him now; suppose she refused his invitation.

There was another thing he had to consider. Suppose one of the gang at the movie made a crack about his father, or about stink bombs. What was he supposed to do then? Even if nobody said anything, Phil knew he would probably think they were just being nice because they had to be.

He got up, walked to the window, and stared out into the growing darkness. Phil thought that no one could ever have felt as alone as he did right now.

Then he saw a shape turn up the sidewalk toward the house. It was Bimbo, and Phil felt better; he didn't feel completely alone anymore. He started for the front door, glad that he had Bimbo to go out to the cave with him.

CHAPTER 12

THE ROAD that ran along the coast was about five miles from Phil's home, and the boys spent the drive discussing what the records would mean once they had them in their possession. Phil explained to Bimbo that Mayor Warford had to keep a set of books on his crooked transactions, even though they could prove damaging. "Graft here in Seacrest is really big business," he said. "They have to keep track of who owes them and how much they've been paid."

They both wondered about Leon Yater. Evidently Warford had trusted the man, for he had Yater keep the secret set of books. Why had Yater defected and run out on Warford? "Maybe he had a change of heart," Bimbo said. "He might have been sick of the way Warford was running things."

"Or more likely because Warford refused to pay him blackmail," Phil said.

"Do you think maybe that's why he took those records? To try and squeeze money out of Warford?"

"I don't know any more about Leon Yater than you do." They agreed that the only thing they actually knew about the accountant was what Jon Hansen had told them. "Hansen said he wasn't a guy you'd cotton up to," Phil said. The boys settled down into silence for some time.

"Did you ask Barbara to go out Friday night?" Phil said suddenly.

"Yeah, why not?"

Bimbo didn't have to worry, Phil thought. "I hope you have a nice time," he snapped.

"I'll give you a full report."

Phil wheeled the car over so quickly that Bimbo was slammed against the door. "What did you do that for?"

"This is our road. I've got to turn when we get to our road, don't I? Why don't you keep your mind on what we're doing, instead of yapping all the time?"

The regular highway cut back from the seashore, but the almost private dirt road Phil had taken ran along the top of the cliffs. Down below them the narrow strand of beach was strung out in both directions, gleaming white in the moonlight.

"We'll have to park the car up ahead," Bimbo said. "There's a path that goes down to the beach. We'll climb up to the cave from there. I don't know whether you can get down from the top or not."

Phil's peevishness disappeared now that they were close to their destination. "You watch for landmarks," he said.

"I remember a lone tree standing next to the path." Bimbo leaned over the wheel to look out. "You'd better slow down."

Phil slowed down and snapped off the headlights. They had no way of knowing what kind of a reception they would get from Leon Yater. He was a desperate man, and a scared one. Phil wished he had asked Virgil Charters whether Yater was armed or not.

"There it is," Bimbo said in a hoarse whisper. "There's the tree."

Phil pulled off the deserted road and stopped. The boys took out the bag of supplies and carried it over to the edge. They started down the steep incline, Phil going down first with one end of the bag, and Bimbo behind him holding the other end. Phil grabbed branches of small brush and held onto rocks to keep from sliding down. Behind him Bimbo was puffing and grunting as he did the same thing.

When they reached the level beach, the boys dropped the bag. "Where is the cave from here?" Phil asked.

Wheezing and puffing, Bimbo pointed to their right, and up the side of the cliff. Phil studied the spot. Back in Charters' office all this had sounded very simple. Go to the cave, hand Leon Yater the supplies, and let him read the note. Out here in the darkness, it was altogether different. The cave Bimbo had pointed out was over halfway up the face of a jagged cliff. There were a mass of boulders and clumps of brush between the beach and the mouth of the cave. Yater could see everything on the beach from the cave, but the boys couldn't even make out the mouth of the cave itself.

"Come on," Phil whispered and swung the bag up over his own shoulder. He grimaced when the cans clanked in the darkness.

The deep sand was like hands trying to hold them back, and Phil had to be careful to keep the cans in the bag from shifting. He felt Bimbo grab his arm, and so he lowered the bag to the ground. "The cave is right above us now," Bimbo whispered.

Phil looked up, but could see even less than he had seen before. He thought of calling out Leon Yater's name, but decided against it. He hoped that if the man was watching them, he would realize the bag was filled with supplies and would be friendly.

The trip back up the face of the cliff was twice as hard as the one coming down had been. They had to move around clumps of brush and climb over boulders. One of the boys would climb up to the next foothold, then pull the bag up. They had to rest often, and though the night air was cool, by the time they had reached the ledge before the cave, both of them were covered with sweat.

Phil stared at the opening ahead. "Mr. Yater," he called softly, "we're friends. We've brought you supplies." He waited, but there was only dead silence from the cave.

Bimbo crawled up beside him. "Is anybody home in there?" he called.

In the stillness, a stab of panic struck Phil. It occurred to him that Yater had disappeared and had taken the records with him. "Mr. Yater," he called urgently, "we brought you supplies." He shook the bag so that the cans clanked. Still there was no movement or sound from the cave.

Phil stood up and advanced cautiously to the opening. The cave wasn't much. As he entered, Phil saw it was little more than a deep crevice with an overhang that sheltered it from above. The cave had one big advantage—it couldn't be seen from either below or above. Phil could almost feel the emptiness inside. He called in once more, and when there was still no answer, he pushed on in, flashlight in hand.

Phil pushed the switch down and swung the beam of light into the cave, across the uneven floor, and to the walls on either side. He advanced cautiously inside and dropped the bag of supplies to the floor.

Bimbo cleared his throat. "I'll bet Warford's men found Yater and took him away," he said.

Bimbo's words expressed Phil's fear. That was the worst thing that could have happened. If Warford's men had found Yater, the records were gone for sure. There would never be a chance they could be used to prove his father was innocent. Phil stubbornly refused to admit that this was what had happened. "We don't know Warford's men found him," he said shortly. "Let's look around here before we jump to any conclusions."

Phil found something close to the wall. He knelt down beside a circle of small stones.

"What is it?" Bimbo said from behind him.

"It's Yater's fire." Phil put his hand down. "The stones are still warm." He picked up a stick and poked around in the ashes until he brought up some glowing coals. "Yater hasn't been gone long," he said, standing up. "At least we know that much."

Phil found something else beside the wall. It was a small heap of supplies Yater had left behind. There were a few tins of canned meat, a plastic bag with three potatoes in it, and a gallon jug, less than half filled with water. "He was lucky we brought him some more stuff," Bimbo said.

"I only hope he comes back to use it." Phil moved on back

into the cave. When the flashlight beam picked out the shape of an old suitcase, he hurried forward, knelt down, and fumbled at the clasp.

"Hey, what are you doing?" Bimbo demanded. "That's personal property."

"Maybe it is," Phil grunted, struggling with the lid, "but if those records are in here, I'm going to take them." He threw the lid back and poked the flashlight beam inside. "This is no time for social niceties."

There was nothing in the suitcase but clothing and toilet articles. Phil fastened the lid and fought back his disappointment as he stood up.

"Maybe Yater hid them around here some place," Bimbo said hopefully.

Phil realized that he had no idea where the records might be. He had assumed that Yater had brought them with him to the cave, but now that he thought back, he wasn't sure Charters had ever said the man had carried them out. Perhaps Charters was as much in the dark as he was and had only guessed that Yater had kept the records on his person. "We'll look around," he said.

The boys searched the cave and the area outside for half an hour before they gave up.

Phil swung the flashlight back into the cave for one last inspection. He considered leaving the note Charters had given him, but decided against that. The supplies they were leaving would tell Yater that they were friends, and if the note were found by someone else, it would incriminate Mr. Charters.

"How about pretending to leave and then hide until Yater comes back?" Bimbo suggested.

"If he was here when we came up the beach, he saw us." Phil kicked at a small stone dejectedly. "In that case, he's hiding out watching us right now. He won't come back here until he's sure we've gone for good."

The boys searched until they found a way to climb onto the top of the cliff. It was difficult, but without the bag of supplies, not so hard as the climb up from the beach. "I guess this explains how Yater got away," Phil said when they stood on top of the cliff. "While we were coming up the beach, he slipped up this way."

"We should have called to him before we did," Bimbo said.

"We should have done a lot of things we didn't do," Phil snapped and turned to walk back to the car. He had been prepared to accept disappointment, but now that their trip was a failure, he was totally crushed. Phil blamed himself. He felt there must have been something he could have done. For the first time he began to doubt his own ability.

The drive back to town was made in glum silence. Phil stopped a block from Bimbo's home to let him out. Bimbo stood with his hand on the door handle for a moment in awkward silence. "Are you sure you don't want to go out on Friday night?" he asked.

Phil looked at him in disgust. "Is that what you've been thinking about?" he demanded. "Is that all you've got to worry about?" Phil turned back to stare through the windshield. "No, I'm not going on any date," he said grimly. Then he put the car in gear and drove off.

Phil went to the hospital the next morning. He hadn't expected to be allowed to see his father, but finding no receptionist at the desk, he decided to go on back. He tapped lightly on the door of room 132.

Miss King gave him a smile. "Dr. Calvin left orders that you might see your father for a few moments," she said, holding the door open. "I'm afraid he can't talk to you," she warned.

Phil nodded. The blinds were drawn against the bright morning sunshine, so the lighting was a soft glow. Carl Martinson lay with his eyes closed, and there was no movement of the body under the sheets. His eyelids were translucent and his face almost as white as the pillow under his head. Phil saw that one arm lay outside the covers, alongside of his father's body. There was a patch of adhesive tape fastened to the inside of the arm, and from this a plastic tube ran up to an inverted glass bottle on a stand.

Miss King had followed Phil to the bed. She nodded in the direction of the bottle. "Your father must be fed intravenously," she said in a low voice. "Even when he's conscious, he refuses to take nourishment."

Phil looked down at his father's still form. He no longer blamed the citizens of Seacrest. After his talk with Dr. Calvin, he understood. He realized that if he had been in their position, he too would have believed as they did. Now he blamed only Mayor Warford and his administration.

Phil left the room and walked slowly out of the hospital. He had made a resolution while he had stood at his father's bedside: he could never doubt his own ability; he had to believe he could accomplish anything. No one else was going to save Carl Martinson—it was up to Phil alone.

Mr. Charters was in his office, waiting, and when Phil entered, the chubby little man bounded to his feet. "Did you see Yater?" he said anxiously. "Did you get those records?"

Phil shook his head to both questions and Charters' face fell. "I didn't even see Yater," Phil said sadly. "If he was there, he took off before I got to the cave." He went on to tell how he had found the suitcase and how the fire still had hot coals.

Charters looked somewhat relieved as he sat down again. "It looks as though our man hasn't completely run out on us then," he said. He looked over at Phil. "I'm disappointed that we weren't able to see him, of course. But I know you must feel a good deal worse about it. I'm sorry."

Phil was grateful for Charters' understanding. The failure to see Yater the night before had been a terrible disappointment to him. "I'm not giving up," he said in a determined voice. "I'm going to talk to Mr. Yater. I intend to go back out there today. I'll stay around that cave until I catch him."

Charters leaned forward. "I understand your impatience," he said. "But that's the wrong approach. If you harass Yater, the man is likely to take off and disappear. Yater trusts no one. He's suspicious of everybody, and hounding him would only make it worse."

Phil bowed his head. "I guess you're right," he said in a low voice. "I might have messed things up again by going off half-cocked."

Charters smiled faintly. "Don't blame yourself too harshly,

son," he said. "Patience comes with maturity." He leaned forward again. "That doesn't mean we're not going to act," he said. "But this next time we must make better preparations."

Phil looked up to see Charters smiling with his lips, but his blue eyes were serious. "You mean I'm to go out to the cave again?" he asked.

Charters nodded and leaned back so that the swivel chair lifted his feet from the floor. He pressed his chubby fingers together and stared at the ceiling. "I told you yesterday that I believed I was being followed," he said thoughtfully. "Well, last night I found out for sure. A car hung close behind me. I made several turns, but the car stayed right behind me. I speeded up and turned into a dark alley. I went back and watched the car go by." He held up his hand to forestall Phil's question. "I think the men in the car were the same thugs who tried to waylay me the other morning," he said.

Phil wasn't surprised that Warford's men were still after Charters. The bold daylight attempt they had made on him proved they were desperate, and there was no reason to think Warford intended to give up. Phil felt a fellowship with Virgil Charters now. "Isn't there someone you can go to for protection?" he asked.

Charters spread his hands. "Who?" he demanded. "Certainly not our local police force. The state police have no jurisdiction unless a state law has been violated. It's the same with the federal authorities." Charters shook his head. "No, son, I'm afraid this is a private fight, and we're going to have to fight it out by ourselves."

"I'm in the same boat," Phil said. "I'm willing to go all the way with you, Mr. Charters. I'll do anything you say."

"Good." Charters let his chair come down with a bump. He reached out and solemnly shook hands with Phil. "Perhaps two heads will be better than one," he said. "Now I've been thinking this problem over while we've been talking, and here's what I've come up with."

Charters went back over the importance of getting their hands on Yater's records. He emphasized that while they could not depend on Leon Yater to testify against Warford, the records themselves would be enough. He stated that he had never actually seen the records and had supposed Yater had them in the suitcase. Now that they weren't there, he imagined Yater had hidden them somewhere around the cave. "I can't see Yater letting those records get very far away from him," Charters said.

"They're not in the cave, but that doesn't mean they can't be somewhere around there."

"I suppose I made a mistake in sending you out alone," Charters went on. "I see now I'll have to go out with you if we expect to see the man. I have to make sure I'm not followed, and I think I have a plan. I have a small speedboat I keep at a sports landing a few miles down the coast. We could come up and land on the beach in front of the cave."

Phil nodded and grinned. "They couldn't very well tail a boat without being spotted."

"It seems almost a foolproof plan," Charters said. "And if there's moonlight, I think Yater will be able to recognize me."

Phil glanced over at Charters' chubby figure and silently

agreed that Yater would know who his visitor was. "When do we go?"

Charters said the trip could be made that evening, and Phil was posed with the problem of telling him about Bimbo. He explained how Bimbo had been with him the night before and asked Charters' permission for him to come again. At first, the man was opposed. "I have nothing against the boy," Charters said. "My opposition is based on the fact that Melton Flood is a constant visitor at the Barnes' home, and if any word of our scheme should leak out around there . . ."

"It won't," Phil said, "I promise you. I'll personally be responsible for Bimbo. I'll see to it he doesn't say a word." With this assurance, Charters agreed that Bimbo could come along, and the final plans for the evening were completed.

Phil left Charters' office in a far more cheerful mood than when he had entered. There were three of them fighting against Mayor Warford—Bimbo, Charters, and himself.

CHAPTER 13

V<small>IRGIL</small> C<small>HARTERS</small> had decided it would be dangerous for the three of them to leave Seacrest together, so he had instructed Phil to take Bimbo to the sports landing while he made the trip in his own car.

Phil did as he had been told, taking a roundabout route, then doubling back on his tracks to make sure he was not being followed. "It looks as if we're in the clear," he told Bimbo once they were on the coast highway. "The sports landing is about ten miles from here."

"Maybe tonight will be the big payoff," Bimbo said, grinning.

"Don't talk like that," Phil warned. "That's the way we talked before, and look what happened."

"Sure, but Charters is handling it this time."

Phil knew how Bimbo felt. Phil had the same feeling—it was a confidence he had never known before in his fight against Warford. Charters was a mature man, one who had already shown his ability by taking precautions. Phil realized that he and Bimbo had been slapdash in the way they had acted before. They had bungled the case like a couple of amateurs. It wasn't surprising that Warford had handled them so easily. From now on it should be different; Charters

was a shrewd businessman and should have some tricks of
his own.

The sports landing was in a cove. Phil pulled off the highway and stopped a short distance from the small, darkened
office. The boys walked down and looked out over the floating dock where the small boats lay padlocked in their slips.
There was no one else around. It was quiet and smooth out
on the water, with moonlight shimmering on the surface.
The only sound that broke the stillness was the gentle lap-
ping of the wavelets against the boats.

Phil stood still, drinking in the calm peacefulness of the
scene before him. He wanted to take one of these boats and
sail on forever. He wanted to forget the dirty business of
Mayor Warford and of his stranglehold on Seacrest. He
wanted to be rid of Leon Yater and of the misery that an
innocent man could suffer because of another's greed.

Phil pulled himself out of his dream with a start. There
was work to be done tonight, and wishing wouldn't accomplish anything.

Both boys looked up with a start when headlights turned
off the highway and took the road down to the sports landing. Phil held his breath when the lights went out and the
car slid to a stop beside his own. He didn't breathe again
until he recognized the chunky figure of Virgil Charters
coming toward them.

Charters was in a cheerful mood. He looked out over the
water and nodded his satisfaction. "It's smooth tonight—
that's good. I'm glad there's a moon. I'm not too sure I could
find the spot without some light." He led the boys down a
flight of steps and out on the floating dock.

He stopped before an eighteen-foot inboard cruiser that had the motor aft and was propelled by a V-drive. "This is a mighty trim-looking craft," Phil said.

Charters thanked him as he opened the padlock that held the boat chained to the mooring. "I take it out during the day," he said, "but this is the first time I've ever had it out at night." He straightened up and pointed over a hill. "The owner of this landing lives over there. I called him this afternoon and told him to have the boat gassed up. I told him I wanted to go out tonight and try my luck."

"I hope your luck's good," Phil said.

Charters had difficulty climbing over the rail. He made a couple of false starts before he tumbled into the cockpit. Bimbo climbed in after him, while Phil untied the painter and coiled the light line in his hand. He threw his weight against the bow, felt the boat moving slowly out of the slip, and he waited until the last moment to leap up on the deck. Then he secured the coiled painter, swung around the low windshield, and dropped down into the cockpit.

Charters and Bimbo had removed the canvas cover from the motor, and Phil helped Bimbo fold and stow the cover under the seat that ran across the boat ahead of the motor. Charters went forward to the wheel and turned the ignition key. It took only a few turns of the starter motor before the boat's power plant burst into life and throbbed with a muffled blast.

The boat drifted aimlessly as Charters allowed the motor to warm up. The exhaust sound had taken on a splutter as water was brought up, pumped through the cooling system, and dumped into the exhaust pipes.

Charters looked back at the boys. "I'll take it easy until we're out in open water," he said in a low voice. He eased the drive into gear, and the boat got slowly under way with the bow pointed toward the open sea.

Phil watched the arms of the cove slide by. He had been willing to let Virgil Charters take charge. He had no intention of questioning any move the man made, and some of Charters' calm assurance seemed to have rubbed off on both Phil and Bimbo.

At the mouth of the cove, Charters pulled back on the throttle. The boat surged ahead with a powerful roar, sending out spume from either side of the bow. Phil dropped into the seat and relaxed. He looked out on the calm ocean and again was seized with the desire to escape. If it hadn't been for his father lying in the hospital, Phil felt he would never return to his home town again. Seacrest seemed far away and unreal out here, and for the first time in over ten days he felt completely at rest.

He turned and looked back. The sea was flat, with no other craft showing. Phil knew Charters was violating the law by being under way without showing running lights, but he could scarcely be expected to use them at a time like this. Phil settled back and thought of what lay ahead of them when they reached the cave. He was confident Charters would get the records once they met Leon Yater.

Phil saw they were running parallel to the shoreline, and he leaned forward to pick out familar landmarks. He searched ahead, hoping to see the lone tree that should stand silhouetted against the sky. With his eyes still shoreward,

Phil took off his shoes and socks. He stuffed the socks into his pocket, while Bimbo did the same thing.

Phil went forward and stood beside Charters. Bimbo saw the tree first. He called out and pointed. Charters nodded, and when they had reached a point directly offshore from the landmark, he swung the boat over to head toward the beach.

The swells built up in closer to shore, and Phil had to hold to the windshield frame as he crawled back up on the forward deck. Charters was holding the boat under half power, and Phil hoped the man knew how to handle a boat under these conditions. Beaching a craft of this size could be tricky business. He unfastened the painter and knelt with the coiled line in his hand.

The boat reached the point where a swell rose to break, and Phil held his breath. If Charters allowed them to broadside in the broken water beyond, they could be swamped. The bow lifted, then dropped, and Phil heard the crash as a breaker exploded against the hull. Charters cut the motor at the last second, but it seemed they were approaching the beach at a tremendous speed.

Phil was poised and ready, and when he heard the hull scrape up on the sand, he leaped overboard. He threshed in through knee-deep water and braced himself on the painter to hold the boat against the outgoing surge of water. Bimbo dropped down and, with both boys pulling and with the help of the next wave, the boat was well beached.

The boys helped Charters clamber down over the bow to the damp sand, where the three of them huddled in a tight cluster. "You stay with the boat, Bimbo," Charters whispered. "Phil and I will go on up to the cave."

The water had been cold, but the sand, still warm from the afternoon sun, felt good to Phil's bare feet as he and Charters walked toward the rocks. "Are you going to call to Yater?" Phil asked when they were close.

"A good idea." Charters stopped, cupped his hand to his mouth and called, "Leon Yater, this is Virgil Charters. I'm coming up."

On the heels of Charters' words a spurt of orange flame stabbed the blackness of the cave mouth. Immediately Phil heard the nasty, snarling whine of a bullet as it ricocheted off a rock before him.

Phil dropped flat on the sand.

More shots were fired from the cave mouth. A quick series of spurts came from the top of the cliff. Bullets were thudding into the sand around them now. "Let's get out of here," Charters said. They jumped up and ran back across the beach.

Halfway back, Charters pitched to the sand. Phil ran back and knelt down beside him. "Are you hit?" he asked anxiously.

"I tripped," Charters gasped and tried to struggle to his feet. Bimbo appeared, and with Charters held between them, the boys ran back to the water line.

It took both of them to boost the chubby man up over the bow and onto the deck. "We've got to get this thing afloat," Phil said, turning and bracing his back against the bow. As he bent, he saw gun flashes coming down the cliff. "They're coming after us. Heave, Bimbo!"

Bimbo leaned his weight against the bow, but at the first shove, it slid back only inches. "One—two—heave!" Bimbo grunted, but their effort failed to budge the boat.

Phil saw that the gunmen had reached the rocks. He bent his back against the hull and planted his feet firmly. "Heave!" he groaned. He felt his stomach muscles pull and the tendons of his legs knot. Slowly the keel began to slide back along the sand. As it moved faster, the boys turned and pushed to keep up the momentum.

They were waist deep in water when the motor burst into life and the boat surged backward. Phil leaped up, caught the rail and held. He hung for an instant, gathering his strength.

Charters had the boat full speed astern when Phil managed to pull himself over the rail. The breakers smashed into the transom, stern on, sending a flood of sea water down into the cockpit with each blow. Phil scrambled around the end of the windshield and onto the deck. He crawled forward, then holding to the bow light for support, he peered down into the water.

Bimbo's head appeared in the churning froth. Phil saw the boy had grabbed the painter, and Phil heaved on the line to pull Bimbo closer. At that moment Charters cut the power suddenly, and with the strain on the line gone, Phil managed to bring Bimbo in close.

The boat had drifted helplessly around when the power was cut. A breaker hit broadside, heeling the boat over until one rail was under water. In that instant, Phil was able to lunge forward and grasp Bimbo's wrists. He held as the boat reared up out of the trough, lifting Bimbo clear.

Charters had the boat under way again and headed out to sea when the boys climbed down into the cockpit. "That was a close call," Charters said without turning his head.

"I'll say it was," Bimbo said through chattering teeth. "You almost left me to drown."

"Wait a minute," Phil said. "If he hadn't let us broadside in front of that breaker, I wouldn't have been able to pull you aboard."

Charters glanced over at Phil, then looked ahead again.

"Maybe so," Bimbo said grudgingly, "but I'm freezing."

"I'm as wet as you are," Phil pointed out. "I don't know what we can do about it." He studied the side of Charters' plump face. He couldn't blame the man for trying to get the boat into deep water, and the way Charters had handled the boat to get Bimbo aboard had taken cool nerve. He decided Charters was a good man to have on his side, even if their mission had been a failure. He fought down his disappointment. "I suppose those were Warford's men up there," he said flatly.

"No doubt about it," Charters said.

"I wonder . . ." Phil had intended to ask how Warford's men had found out about the cave. But suddenly he knew how they had found out. There wasn't any other explanation—he hadn't told anyone about their going out to the cave the night before, but he hadn't taken any precautions against being followed, either. The men who had been following Charters had seen Phil at the mill. They had put a tail on him and had followed the boys out to the cave.

He himself had led Warford's men to Yater last night.

Bimbo was wringing water out of his trousers. "Do-do-do

you suppose they murdered Yater?" he asked through chattering teeth.

The experience hadn't shaken Charters. When he turned, his expression was calm. "I don't know," he said. "I do know one thing," he went on. "We've lost all chance to get the records."

Phil knew Charters had figured out how Warford's men had found the cave, but his words had not been an accusation. Charters hadn't made it sound that way. His tone had been matter-of-fact, entirely without bitterness.

Phil huddled against the side and felt miserable. If Charters had only taken charge last night, instead of tonight.

The boat was returned to the slip, and the three of them stood beside the office building. "No post-mortems." Charters gave them a wave and walked to his car.

"What did he mean by that crack?" Bimbo asked, looking after Charters.

"He meant not to blame ourselves for what happened tonight."

"Blame ourselves?" Bimbo said indignantly. "It wasn't our fault—he was running things. He was the one who gave us the dunking. What does the guy mean—blame ourselves?"

"If you don't know, forget it," Phil said wearily. "Let's get home. I want to get into some dry clothes."

Phil dropped Bimbo off, and when he turned into his own driveway, he didn't notice the car parked under a tree on the street. He was too cold and miserable to notice anything.

Phil put his car away and pulled the garage door down. When he started up the path to the back door, two men materialized out of the darkness. "Hold it right there," one of the men said.

Phil bristled with anger when he saw the man was the tall plainclothesman who had held him and Bimbo prisoner at the civic auditorium. "What do you want?" Phil demanded.

The man's shorter companion had joined him. "Come along with us to city hall," the man said. He grabbed Phil's arm.

Phil pulled back. "I'm wet," he said. "Let me get into some other clothes first. I'm freezing."

"You should have taken them off before you went swimming. Come on, we haven't got all night."

Phil looked toward his house. The light burned in the front room. Mrs. Flemming always left that light on when he or his father was out. He realized he would gain nothing by trying to argue. He had learned that these men wouldn't hesitate to use force. The shorter man was already moving in. "All right," he said bitterly, "you're the police."

The short man drove, while the tall man sat with Phil in the back seat. They did not speak, and Phil made no attempt at conversation. He didn't try to guess why he was being taken to city hall. He was too uncomfortable to think.

The car pulled up behind the building, and Phil was rushed through a rear door. He had never been in this section before, and he wondered if Jon Hansen was somewhere out in front. They climbed a flight of stairs, and at the top landing, the short man stuck his head through a door before he looked back and motioned them on. The tall man went ahead, rapped on a door down the hall, and then opened it and pushed Phil into the room.

Mayor Warford dominated the room, even though he was seated behind a desk. His iron-gray hair was rumpled, his coat hung on a chair back, and his shirt collar was open. Warford stared at Phil, while Phil glared back at Mayor Warford. There was nothing to the old notion that a guilty man couldn't look you straight in the eye, Phil thought. Mayor Warford could.

Warford finally broke the silence. "So we meet again," he said in his deep rumble.

"I only want to know one thing. Am I under arrest?"

"You're not under arrest. I sent for you because I wanted to have a little talk."

Sent for me, Phil thought angrily. He'd been dragged down here. He started to mention his wet clothes, but decided against that when he thought Warford probably knew all about the shooting on the beach. The mayor looked as though he had been waiting here all evening. "I'm listening," Phil said.

"How is your father?" Mayor Warford said abruptly.

Phil felt his face redden. He clenched his fists and took a step forward. He was grabbed by the tall plainclothesman. "You know how he is," Phil said angrily. "You ought to know—you put him there."

Warford's expression remained calm. He had asked the question for a purpose. He had received the desired result, and he was beyond letting personal insults affect him. "I understand he's in bad shape," Warford said. "Another blow could be too much for a man in his condition." Warford clasped his hands on the desk and looked at Phil from under lowered lids. "You have persisted in trying to annoy me lately, and I'm about fed up."

"I intend to make you a lot more fed up," Phil said tersely.

"I've taken all I intend to take." Warford paused to let his remark have the full effect. Phil heard the tall man behind him shuffle his feet. Phil looked defiantly back into the mayor's eyes and waited. "Until lately you were nothing but an annoyance," Warford went on in the same tone. "But when you tied up with Virgil Charters, you tried to move up to the big league, son. You can get hurt bad trying to play with the big boys—you'd better think that over."

"I can take care of myself," Phil said.

Mayor Warford rose, placed his palms flat on the desk, and leaned forward. "Where are those records Leon Yater stole from me?" he demanded in a steel-hard voice.

The question hit Phil with a terrific impact. It was so unexpected that he was left confused. He tried to gather his thoughts before he framed a reply. He couldn't ask, What records? That would sound childish. "I don't know where they are," he said.

Mayor Warford sighed heavily and sat down. "I had hoped you would see the light," he said wearily.

The tall man cleared his throat. "Maybe if we took him . . ."

Warford shook his head. "No, he's a kid, and that would look bad."

"But . . ." the tall man said.

Warford raised his hand. "I'm not through with him yet." He turned back to Phil. "You're bringing this on yourself," he said evenly. "I'm forced to go to the district attorney and ask for an indictment against your father on criminal charges."

"A thing like that would kill him," Phil said weakly.

"That's your worry."

"I don't know where those records are."

The muscles in Warford's jaw hardened. The cords on his neck stood out. It was obvious that he was struggling to hold on to his self-control. He closed his eyes, then opened them again; but a thin veil still seemed to be drawn across his eyeballs. "You said that before," he said in a strained voice. "I think you're a liar."

"And you'll be a murderer!" Phil lunged forward as he shouted. The tall man threw his right arm around Phil's neck and jerked back. Phil felt a terrible pain in his throat and down through his chest. Spots flickered before his eyes as he struggled for a breath of air.

"Let him go," Mayor Warford said.

Phil sucked in air when the tall man released his hold. Flashes of light still jabbed before his eyes as he rubbed his throat. "I don't . . ." he finally managed to gasp.

"If those records aren't in my hands by tomorrow noon," Warford said, ignoring Phil's protest, "I'm going to the district attorney. That's my final word." He looked beyond Phil. "Take him out the back way and turn him loose."

Phil trudged through the streets on his way home. His throat was brutally bruised on the outside and raw inside. Pain contorted his face when he swallowed. And he knew he was powerless to prevent Warford from going through with his threat.

There was little satisfaction in knowing now that Warford's men hadn't been able to get those records at the cave, for the records would have no value to Phil if his father died. He wondered if he would turn the records over to Warford to save his father's life. He shook his head and stumbled on. There was no point in wondering that—he didn't have the records.

Phil thought briefly about Leon Yater's fate. Yater was a stranger; Phil had never met him. He was someone Phil had only heard about—but Carl Martinson was his father.

CHAPTER 14

THE NEXT MORNING Phil waited in the parking lot next to the building where Dr. Calvin had his office. When the doctor drove in, Phil walked over to his car. He gave none of the details of the night before, but stated that Mayor Warford had threatened to bring criminal charges against his father. "How would that affect my father's condition?" he asked.

The doctor's eyes were troubled. "I can't say—one can never be sure . . ."

Phil saw that it would be difficult to get a direct answer. "Would he understand what those charges were?" he asked.

Dr. Calvin compressed his lips. He looked away, then back to Phil. "I'm going to talk straight to you, son. I'll try to give you the facts in the best way I can." Then in simple, straightforward language, he said that there were periods when Carl Martinson could comprehend. If he were told about the charges during one of those periods, the shock could be enough to cause his death.

"You mean he just wouldn't want to live anymore," Phil said slowly.

"Carl Martinson is a man of strong moral convictions," Dr.

Calvin said. "In his mind there are certain things that are worse than death."

Phil left the parking lot convinced of one thing. He couldn't stop the mayor, but he had to keep them from reaching his father.

Phil decided not to work at the studio that morning. He hoped Scotty would understand. Phil sat in his car and tried to outline some course of action.

With all his other troubles, he was now faced with financial problems. The bills had been mounting at an alarming rate during the past week. There would be Dr. Calvin's bill, the private nurses must be paid, and so must Mrs. Flemming. And there was the regular household budget, of course.

Phil had a savings account. He had opened it when he was a small boy and added to it through the years, always with the thought that it wouldn't be touched until he went to college. "Well, I'm not going to college now," he said as he walked into the bank.

He next went to the old feed and grain mill to tell Charters how he had been taken to Mayor Warford's office. The office door was locked, and on impulse Phil walked around to the side to peer through the dust-covered windows of the double door. He shaded his eyes, but the window was too dirty and streaked to enable him to make out anything in the murky interior.

A thought had nagged at Phil since the night before, when he had found that Mayor Warford didn't have the records. This meant Yater hadn't kept the records around the cave. If they had been in his home, the search there would have revealed them. Phil knew of only one other place Leon Yater had been—the mill. Charters had said Yaters had hidden his car here in the back of the mill.

Phil felt guilty over the failure of the mission the night before and he wanted to do something to atone for his carelessness. He could tell Virgil Charters he thought the records might be hidden in Yater's car—or he could find those papers and take them to Charters.

Phil walked around to where the spur railroad track ran along the rear of the mill. Most of the windows on this side had been broken by vandals and now were boarded up. Down near the end, Phil found one window with the top pane broken, but with no boards nailed across the opening. He found wooden crates, piled them up, and managed to reach the catch through the broken pane. When he had the window open, he crawled in.

He found himself in a small room that had probably been used to store material. Now it was completely empty. Dust covered everything, and where the diagonal beam of light from the window struck the floor, there was a square patch of glistening dust, just as it had settled there, undisturbed for the past ten years.

Phil stood silently in the center of the room to get his bearings. A sudden scurrying sound outside in the mill gave him a start. "Rats," he said in a relieved tone when he realized that a feed mill would be a haven for rodents. Even after all these years, there would still be enough grain around to keep them fed. The floorboards creaked when he crossed over and opened the door.

Phil found himself in a huge open space. It was a room of

cathedral-like silence, and the irregular pattern of sunlight that streamed through the boarded openings gave somewhat the effect of stained glass windows.

The big room somehow seemed familiar; then it came to Phil that he had been here before, only at the other end, when he had driven in to pick up the supplies. He was able now to make out the shape of the double doors on the far side.

Phil looked around and decided that the only possible place an automobile could be hidden was under the stack of cardboard cartons piled high in one corner. He pulled the cartons away and found Yater's old coupé. Methodically he began his search, going through every place the records might be concealed. He was dusty and discouraged when he finally put the front seat back into place. The records hadn't been hidden in Yater's car.

Phil replaced the cartons, crossed the room, and opened another door. This room was smaller than the one Phil had left, but instead of being empty, there was a row of heavy machinery down the middle. Phil looked down the line; he recognized grinders and blowers, but the other machinery was unfamiliar to him. The huge iron machines stood mute, just as they had on that day when a workman had cut off their power for the last time.

A feeling of depression settled down over Phil as he walked back to the storage room and climbed out of the window. There had been no real reason for him to think he would find anything, he told himself. He was grasping at straws, and there were bound to be disappointments working that way.

Phil went to the studio, after all. He explained his absence and Scotty merely nodded. Several times during the morning, Phil was on the verge of telling Scotty about Leon Yater and of his trip to Warford's office. He wanted to ask Scotty's advice on how to protect his father. Each time Phil held back and said nothing. Scotty seemed to have grown cool and aloof during the past few days.

Phil intended to take money over to the nurse at the hospital, and on the way he decided to stop and pick up something for his father. As he walked into Barnes Department Store, he told himself he wasn't taking a present to make up for his failures, but he wondered if that wasn't the real reason. In the men's department he selected a pair of pajamas.

He was waiting for his parcel when he heard his name called. He turned to see Melton Flood approaching. "Hello there, Phil," the young man said, putting out his hand.

Phil felt self-conscious shaking hands with Flood. Samuel Barnes' assistant had never been friendly to him before, and after Charters had voiced his suspicions of the man, Phil felt uneasy trying to be polite. He shook hands briefly and was glad when the clerk handed him his package so he could turn away. "I bought a little present for my father," he said. "I'm on my way to the hospital now." He hoped Flood would take the hint and let him get away.

"Phil," Flood said, taking hold of Phil's arm, "I've been wanting to talk to you. What I have to say won't take long," he added quickly. "We could go up to my office."

Phil hesitated. If Flood had some reason to talk, Phil would be a fool not to listen. Remembering that he was grasping at straws now, he nodded. "I guess I can spare a few minutes."

Flood led the way up to the mezzanine floor and opened the door to a small office. "It isn't much," Flood said, smiling faintly. "I expect to do better."

Phil remembered that he had heard Samuel Barnes was grooming Flood to manage the store. "It looks fine to me," he said.

Flood closed the door and crossed over to his desk. He draped one leg over the edge and folded his arms in what Phil took to be a pose of relaxed friendliness. "I was very sorry to hear about your father's illness," he said.

Phil wondered if this remark was being used as an opening wedge. "Thank you," he said.

Flood unfolded his arms and studied his fingernails. "You probably know that I'm active in the Citizens' Protective League," he said.

"I've heard you were."

"First, I owe you an apology for the other morning in Scotty Kendall's studio," Flood said, as though he had decided to make a fresh start. "I'm afraid I was rather rude when you wanted to play that tape recording. You see, we were pretty busy here at the store and . . ."

"I understand. The thing was a dud anyway."

"I've done a great deal of thinking about that recording and what you were trying to do." Flood looked at Phil with a tight little smile of approval. "I'm afraid I didn't take you seriously enough, young fellow."

Flood's attempt at hearty friendship bothered Phil. He

was sure the man had something on his mind. "I'm glad someone appreciates me," he said quietly.

"I'll admit that the Citizens' League hasn't been too active in the past," Flood went on. "There was internal conflict—some of the members were suspicious of each other and their motives. But now I think we have eliminated those who caused the conflict." Flood looked up and smiled again. "From now on I think we're going to make real progress."

Phil supposed Flood was talking about Virgil Charters. He still didn't see what Flood was driving at, but decided not to commit himself. "I hope so," he said.

"Now I know that because of your father's position, you have been working . . ." He paused a minute and then added, "As long as we're both trying to achieve the same ends, I thought perhaps it would be a good idea to pool what information we have." Flood stopped and looked up.

Phil stared at Flood. "You mean you want me to tell you what I've found out about Mayor Warford?"

"Yes," Flood said, "I feel it would be mutually beneficial."

Phil was wary. He thought of what Charters had said about Flood. He certainly had no intentions of giving the man any information, but if he didn't refuse flat out, he might learn something. Phil found it hard not to say what was in his mind, but he held back. "I don't know," he said cautiously. "What kind of information can I expect the Citizens' League to give me?"

Before Flood could answer, the door opened and Samuel Barnes entered. He hesitated. Then when he saw Phil, he came on in. "I'm sorry if I'm interrupting anything," he said.

"I was just leaving, Mr. Barnes," Phil said.

Barnes stroked his jaw. "I'm sorry about your father, son," he said gruffly. "I'm blamed sorry. I've known Carl Martinson a long time."

"Dad is pretty sick," Phil said quietly.

Mr. Barnes started to turn away, then turned back. "Buford's mother is pretty upset at some of his shenanigans," he said. Phil didn't answer. He didn't feel he had to apologize for Bimbo. Barnes didn't seem to think a reply was necessary. "Not that I blame you too much," he went on. "Buford's mother thinks he can't get into trouble by himself. I know better." He waved his fist in the air. "If there's any devilment to be thought up, that boy can think it up himself."

"Mr. Barnes," Flood said hurriedly, "Buford will be leaving Seacrest soon to go to school. That should solve everything."

Samuel Barnes lowered his arm. "I guess it will," he said and walked to the desk. "What I came in here for was to see if you got confirmation on that shipment of bedsheets."

"Yes, sir, I have it right here." Flood hurried around and pulled a sheaf of papers from a desk drawer. Phil left the room while the two men were bent over the papers.

On the way to the hospital, Phil went over Flood's proposition. If the man was working for the Citizens' League, as he claimed, then why had he shut up suddenly when Samuel Barnes entered the office? Barnes was the head of the League—he would certainly be interested if any deal was going to be made.

Phil arrived at the hospital undecided about what Flood's

real intention had been. But he was sure of one thing—he wasn't going to tell the man anything.

Miss King stepped out of the door of room 132 and closed it softly behind her. She told Phil his father was asleep. He decided not to go in—it was too depressing to see his father when he was unable to talk. "I brought these for him," he said, holding out the package. "They're pajamas."

Miss King took the pajamas, and after Phil had arranged her wages, he frowned. "You wouldn't let anyone else get in to see my father?" he asked.

Miss King's eyes were steady. "You are the only one allowed in," she said.

"Sure, but I mean if someone tried to get . . ."

"Dr. Calvin told me about it this morning," she said in a calm professional tone. "He left orders that no one was to get close to your father."

Phil felt reassured as he left. The cool efficiency of the young nurse, and the foresight of Dr. Calvin made him feel sure his father was well guarded.

Phil spent some time at the studio before he went home. Bimbo didn't show up all afternoon, and Phil wondered about this. Then, that evening at dinner, he remembered that it was Friday and Bimbo had a date. He had more important things to think about than Phil's problems. "Darn him," he said aloud. "I hope he chokes on a malt after the movie."

Mrs. Flemming looked over in shocked horror. "What did you say?" she demanded.

Phil mumbled into his napkin. He reached into his pocket

and pulled out his billfold. He took out bills and tossed them on the table. "Here's some money to run the house on," he said. "You take your wages out of it, too."

Mrs. Flemming drew her plump little figure upright. "Just put that money back into your pocket, young man. I don't need it."

"But we have bills to pay," Phil said impatiently.

"The bills are being paid on time. We're doing quite nicely, thank you."

"But you can't use your own money to pay the bills," Phil protested.

Mrs. Flemming gave Phil a haughty stare. "And I should like to know why not?" she said. "Has someone else a better right than I have? You run things on the outside—you tend to your knitting, and I'll tend to mine."

Phil picked up the bills and replaced them in his billfold. He got up and walked around to stand beside Mrs. Flemming's chair. He leaned down, and for the first time in quite a while, he kissed her on the cheek.

Mrs. Flemming turned to look up at Phil. Her eyes were large as she reached up and felt the spot he had kissed. "Thank you, Phillip," she said quietly. "Thank you very much."

Phil tried to watch television for the next hour, but he could find nothing to hold his interest. No matter what happened on the screen, his thoughts went somewhere else. Finally he gave up and snapped off the switch, put on his jacket, and went out to his car. A drive would help to straighten him out, he thought.

Phil came out on Ramona Road, and strung out before

him lay the jungle of lights that was the neon badge of shame for Seacrest. The dives along that road were allowed to stay open only because they paid Mayor Warford to let them operate. No wonder he needed a man like Leon Yater to keep a record of pay-offs. If Melton Flood was sincere when he said the Citizens' League wanted information on Mayor Warford, all they would have to do was to come out here on Ramona Road—Warford's guilt was strung up and down for a mile, in lighted letters two feet tall.

Phil thought of all the decent, honest citizens of Seacrest who never came to Ramona Road, who probably hated what it represented. Why did they allow it to exist? It was in their power to wipe it out, but little had been done so far. Scotty had said the people of Seacrest were apathetic. All it would take to drive Warford out of town would be to vote him out of office. Each citizen over twenty-one owned a vote. Why didn't he use it?

Phil drove back through town. His trip out to Ramona Road had left him more downcast than ever. He felt he must talk to someone—anyone. He remembered how close he had come to telling Scotty everything today, and he swung over to drive by the studio.

There was a light on in the studio office, and Phil felt relieved as he pulled up and parked. Tonight he would tell Scotty about Leon Yater, about the records, and about Warford's threat to have his father indicted.

Phil felt a let-down when he approached the door and heard the murmur of voices inside. Scotty had visitors. The shade on the front door was drawn down halfway, so Phil could see only the floor as far as Scotty's desk. He hesitated, then knocked.

The sound of voices ceased abruptly. Phil saw a pair of men's legs—from the knee down—cross the office and disappear. There was silence before Scotty opened the door. "Oh, it's you," Scotty said, but made no move to swing the door open.

It was impossible for Phil to enter without forcing his way in. "I . . ." he began, "I came back after my camera," he said lamely.

"I'll get it for you." Scotty turned and went into the darkroom. He had left the door partially open, and Phil saw that the office was empty. The visitor had gone into the darkroom when Phil had knocked. Scotty returned a moment later. "Here you are," he said.

"Thanks," Phil said, taking the camera, "thanks a lot." He heard the latch click firmly behind him as he turned away.

Phil puzzled over Scotty's strange actions all the way home. Scotty had always been cynical and sometimes abrupt, but Phil had never known him to be deliberately rude before. He had given Phil the brush-off, but good. Scotty had shown he didn't want Phil around—at least not tonight.

Phil was bewildered and hurt by Scotty's actions. As he put his car in the garage, he began to wonder who would come to the studio to visit Scotty at this hour. It was someone who didn't want to be seen there, that was evident enough.

A disturbing thought began to stir in Phil's brain. He felt it was impossible to recognize a man by seeing him only from the knees down, yet, somehow, he had the feeling that he had seen Scotty's visitor before. Perhaps it was the walk, he thought. But he had seen the legs for only a few seconds, and he couldn't remember anything distinctive about the walk.

Phil was halfway to the house when the thought finally broke through his subconscious and burst into full bloom. Phil stopped dead still. He couldn't believe it—he couldn't believe what he had seen back there in the studio. The feet that had walked across the floor had worn alligator shoes, and the only pair of alligator shoes Phil had ever seen had been worn by Mayor Warford!

CHAPTER 15

Phil spent a fitful night. Several times he awakened, and each time he was bathed in sweat, with the bedclothes twisted around him. He could remember visions of being in the hospital room, trying to defend his father, while Scotty Kendall and Mayor Warford did a war dance outside the window. Miss King had been trying to hold the door against a horde of screaming citizens and Bimbo had sat on the floor, yelling with laughter.

Even a tingling shower did little for Phil the next morning. He was able to eat only a few bites of cereal. Then he went into the front room and dropped into the easy chair. He didn't even consider going into the studio.

When the doorbell rang and Mrs. Flemming ushered Bimbo into the room, Phil grunted a greeting. Bimbo slumped down in the other chair and the boys sat in glum silence. Finally Phil looked up. "I suppose you had a ball last night," he said. "Did the gang rake me over the coals plenty?"

"How would I know?" Bimbo said in a low voice. "On the way out of the movie, I heard one stupid crack, and not being the kind to break furniture over stupid people's heads, we skipped the malt shop."

180

Phil stared at Bimbo. "You didn't eat? I can't believe it." A sudden warmth filled his chest. "You're a lunkhead, Bimbo Barnes." He jumped out of his chair and landed on Bimbo. He swung his fists into Bimbo's ribs. Both boys fell heavily together, and pummeled each other as they rolled across the floor.

Mrs. Flemming came in on the run and stopped short when she saw Phil and Bimbo. "Boys," she said weakly, "boys." She watched them for a minute before she shook her head in bewilderment and left the room.

Bimbo gave up first. He rolled over on his back, gasping for breath.

Phil lay on the floor beside him, his arms outstretched. "What a goofball I drew in you," he said.

"Knucklehead," Bimbo panted.

Now that he felt he had Bimbo back, a great deal of the misery he had felt since the night before dissolved. Phil could think clearly again, and face what was before him. He got to his feet and dropped into the easy chair again. "Come on, get up," he told Bimbo, "or Mrs. Flemming will sweep you out with the rest of the trash."

Phil hadn't seen Bimbo since the night of the cruise, so he brought him up to date on all the happenings since then. He saved the part about seeing the alligator shoes until last. When he told of his suspicions, Bimbo's mouth dropped open. "You mean you think Scotty had Mayor Warford in his office?" he gasped. "You're kidding."

"I'm not kidding. If you had seen the way Scotty acted, you'd understand."

"I can't believe it."

Phil pointed his finger at Bimbo. "Have you ever seen any man other than Mayor Warford wearing alligator shoes?"

Bimbo shook his head. "I don't think my father even has a pair in his store. But I stopped by the studio this morning to see if you were there. Scotty seemed the same as always."

"Sure he did. That's why we've never suspected him."

Bimbo stared at the floor. "Are you going to keep working there?" he asked.

"No!"

"I think it might be a good idea," Bimbo said. "If Scotty really is in with Warford, you might be able to pick up some information by hanging around Scotty."

"I couldn't do it," Phil said grimly. "I couldn't face Scotty and act polite if I thought he might be one of the men who put Dad in the hospital. I'm not built that way, Bimbo."

"I guess maybe you're right. You know, Scotty could even be King Rooster."

"He could," Phil snapped. "He knew about that tape recording. He knew we were going to that public forum. About the only thing we can't pin on him is what happened out there at the cave."

Bimbo looked up, startled. "Did you ever tell Scotty about Leon Yater?" he asked.

"No, but I almost did. That's why I stopped by the studio last night. I was all set to spill everything right into his lap."

Bimbo said, "Let's figure things out and see who's on Warford's side, and who's on ours."

"After last night, I believe everybody is on his side," Phil said.

"OK, that should make it an even fight. You and me against everybody else."

The boys discussed what had happened. They started back eleven days before, when the wall had collapsed. They talked about each suspect and tried to decide whom they could trust. They were agreed that Mayor Warford was so desperate to get hold of the records that he had tipped his hand to Phil. This was something he had never done before. They had no idea whether Yater was dead or alive, but they had to assume he was dead. In either case, it seemed that the records were gone forever, and that was to Warford's advantage, not theirs.

"Whoever ends up with those records will have the grand prize," Bimbo said.

They then discussed the possible places Yater might have hidden the records. They agreed they hadn't been left in his house, and now they were sure he hadn't taken them to the cave. "I searched his car," Phil said. "They're not there."

"By the way," Bimbo said, "what do these records look like, anyway?"

Phil stared at him. "I don't know," he said slowly. "I guess they might be in some kind of a ledger or maybe some pages out of a ledger. They're a bunch of figures that bookkeepers use to keep track of money paid in and out."

"I just wondered what we were looking for," Bimbo said, then grinned. "Maybe he hid them in the cemetery. Yater was nuts about that place."

"We can't go around digging up graves."

"How about that marble house in there?"

"You mean the mausoleum?" Phil scratched his head. "I've

never been in there, but it's a chance. We'll put that on our list."

"Me and my big fat mouth."

Phil went back over his conversation with Melton Flood. He questioned Bimbo, but found that Bimbo actually didn't know anything about the man. Flood had come to work for the store straight out of college, and Samuel Barnes was quite impressed with the young man's drive. Bimbo didn't care much for the man, but Phil thought the fact that Barnes held Flood up as an example of industry might account for some of Bimbo's distaste. Phil suggested Bimbo should hang around the store and learn more about Flood.

"You don't know what you're asking," Bimbo wailed. "Dad would put me to work in the stock room. He does it every time he catches me in the store."

"That might not hurt you. At least you could talk to some of the other employees, and they must have some opinions about Flood."

In spite of Bimbo's protests, Phil took him down to the department store and dropped him off. After leaving Bimbo, Phil drove to the hospital.

Miss King gave Phil a bright smile when she opened the door of room 132. "Your father will be glad to see you," she said.

"Is he—he—awake?"

Miss King nodded. "He certainly is," she said. "He had a very good night, and this morning he's as chipper as a sparrow." Miss King glanced down at her wristwatch. "You didn't see my relief when you came by the desk, did you? I haven't had breakfast yet."

"You go ahead," Phil told her. "I'll stay with Dad until you get back." He was glad of the chance to be alone with his father. Miss King promised not to be gone long.

The room was bright. Sunshine streamed through the window, and Phil seemed to feel a new hope in the air. His father followed Phil with his eyes as he crossed to the bed.

"Good morning, Dad," Phil said.

His father wore the new pajamas. He had a fresh shave, and Phil thought there was more color in his cheeks. "Hello, son," Carl Martinson's voice was clear, but it was so faint that Phil moved closer.

"You look great, Dad."

"I feel better."

Phil stood in embarrassed silence. He had waited all week for a chance to talk to his father, and now he could think of nothing to say. There wasn't much he could talk about—he couldn't tell about working with Virgil Charters or anything about Leon Yater. He wanted to avoid any mention of Mayor Warford. His father had come up from a deep abyss. He had only a faint grasp on reality, and a misstep could plunge him back down again. "How do you like the pajamas?" he asked.

His father reached up and stroked the lapel. "Pretty gay," he said. "How are things at home?"

"Fine," Phil said heartily. "They're just fine. Everything's going along smoothly. We're just waiting for you to get back."

His father frowned slightly, as though he were trying to think or capture a fleeting worry. "How long have I been here?"

"Gosh, I don't know." Phil counted back. "Five days, I think. But you're not going to be here much longer—not the way you're improving."

His father shook his head to clear the mental cobwebs. "The bills," he said. 'They must be mounting up. I haven't written any checks."

"Don't you worry about bills, Dad. Everything's under control, I promise you that. Do you know what Mrs. Flemming did? She made me let her pay the household bills out of her own pocket—how about that?"

His father still frowned. "I'll repay her."

"Sure, sure, you can. You can do that later—but wasn't that a kick? Mrs. Flemming sends her best wishes; she'll come here as soon as they'll let her come."

"I'll be glad to see her," his father said and closed his eyes. He remained silent for a moment before he looked up at Phil. "How are things going, son? I mean the matter about . . ."

"Nothing to worry about," Phil said quickly. "Everything is going along smooth as glass."

His father shook his head. "But the wall—the accident."

"Now you take it easy and forget that," Phil said. "I promise you there's nothing for you to worry about. There wasn't even an investigation." Phil knew he had promised never to lie to his father, but now he felt he was justified. He had told a half-truth—there never had been a formal inquiry. "You just lie there and get back on your feet." He turned when there was a rapping on the door. "Come in," he called.

A young man stepped in. He was dressed in the white

shirt and trousers of a hospital aide. He hesitated when he saw Phil. "Mr. Martinson?" he asked.

"I'm Phil Martinson. This is my father." Phil remembered what Miss King had said outside the door. "Were you supposed to relieve Miss King?"

The young man nodded. "I'm sorry, I was held up. I have a message for you, Mr. Martinson. Dr. Calvin said that if you were here, he wanted to see you at once, that it was urgent. He's in the chief's office now."

"Urgent?" Phil wondered why Dr. Calvin hadn't come back to the room if he thought Phil might be there. Then he realized that the matter must be something the doctor wanted kept from his father. Phil was angry at the young aide for blurting this out, but it was too late to worry about that.

"I'm free now," the young man said. "I can stay with the patient until Miss King returns."

Phil leaned over his father. "I'm sorry, Dad. I'll drop in again before I leave." He placed his hand over his father's veined hand.

"I'll be all right now, son. Don't you worry."

Phil asked the receptionist for the Chief of Staff's office and was directed down a short corridor. He found the door and knocked. There was no response from inside and he knocked again, impatiently. A sudden chilling fear seized Phil and he opened the door. The room was empty.

Phil ran back down the corridor to the reception desk. No, the girl there knew nothing about any message from Dr. Calvin. In fact, Dr. Calvin hadn't been in the hospital that morning.

Phil was racing down the hall when he saw that the door of room 132 was open. His father lay with his head thrown back. His eyes were closed, and his skin was a dull ashen gray. His right arm hung over the side of the bed, and Phil's eyes traveled on down the arm, over the fingertips, and to the floor. He knelt down and picked up a paper from under his father's limp hand. The paper was a warrant, and though tears of rage welled up to blur Phil's vision, he made out the word *Manslaughter*.

Slowly he turned and saw Miss King in the doorway.

The nurse looked at her patient and hurried across the room. "Get a staff doctor," she said. Phil started for the door, still clutching the paper. "Have them call Dr. Calvin," Miss King added. "This is an emergency."

Phil was not allowed to enter his father's room again. He spent the next half hour pacing the waiting room. Miss King had been efficient. Dr. Calvin had taken all precautions, but Phil had blundered. He had been duped—sucked in by a process server disguised as a hospital aide.

Phil saw Dr. Calvin coming up the front walk. As soon as the doctor entered, Phil shoved the paper at him. "It was my fault Dad saw it," Phil said brokenly. "I thought the man worked here at the hospital."

Dr. Calvin scanned the paper briefly. He handed it back and walked grimly down the hall toward room 132.

Phil had no idea how long he wrestled with his own remorse, and his fear, before Dr. Calvin returned. "You can blame me . . ." he began, but Dr. Calvin cut him short.

"I have no time for accusations or self-pity," he said. "Your father has received a severe shock, but he is still alive."

Phil realized he had the rebuke coming, and the relief of hearing his father was alive swept away any resentment against the doctor. "How is he?"

Dr. Calvin's expression softened and his voice was kind when he spoke. "We discussed this probability before, son," he said. "I'm afraid it's going to be about what we feared."

"You mean he won't want to live?"

"Something like that." The doctor put his hand on Phil's shoulder. "Forget about that process server, Phil," he said. "Blaming yourself isn't going to help your father any, and it could do a lot of harm."

Phil thought over Dr. Calvin's words as he left the hospital. He knew the doctor meant that if Phil spent his time blaming himself, he wouldn't be able to get anything else done. He made a silent resolution that from now on he would think only of the future and his father's health, not the past and his own mistakes.

Phil called Mrs. Flemming into the front room and told her about his father's condition. She stood in shocked silence, wringing her hands in her apron as she listened. "Oh, the poor man," she said brokenly.

Phil hadn't given any details, and he had purposely accused no one. He felt it was better not to clutter up Mrs. Flemming's mind with anything but concern over his father's condition. "I'll keep in touch with Dr. Calvin," he said, "That's about all we can do."

Mrs. Flemming's eyes filled with tears. "And pray," she added.

"Yes, and pray," Phil said soberly.

Phil was on his way to his room when Mrs. Flemming

called him back. "I just remembered," she said. "With all this terrible news and all, it slipped my mind. Jon Hansen has been calling here for you ever since you left."

"Mr. Hansen? You're sure?"

"That's who he said he was," Mrs. Flemming said. "He's mighty anxious to get in touch with you."

"Did he mention what he wanted?"

Mrs. Flemming put her stubby forefinger against her cheek while she frowned in furious thought. "He did say something—it seems to me he mentioned a man's name. Yes, I'm sure. It will come to me." The housekeeper's face beamed with personal satisfaction. "He said he wanted to talk to you about Leon Yater."

CHAPTER 16

J ON HANSEN must have called from a pay telephone, for Phil could not find his name listed in the book. Luckily, Phil knew where the custodian lived and drove to the street lined with modest cottages.

Hansen must have been waiting on the porch, for he was down the front walk and out of the gate before Phil could get out of his car. "My wife's pretty nervous," Hansen explained through the car window. "She upsets easy, so maybe we'd better talk out here."

Phil wondered if the real reason wasn't that Hansen didn't want the neighbors to see Phil Martinson calling at the Hansen home. "Sure," he said, "this is as good as anywhere. You said you knew something about Leon Yater."

"It happened last night," Hansen said. "I get off work at midnight, and I was driving home. The streets are pretty well deserted at that time of the morning," he added.

Phil realized that in spite of his impatience, he couldn't speed the old man up. Hansen would tell the story in his own rambling way. "Yes," he said, "I know."

"Well, that was why I noticed this man, skulking along."

"Along where, Mr. Hansen?" Phil asked patiently.

"Along First Street," Hansen replied. "Well, there was

191

something about this fellow's size and walk that made me want to have a second look at him. Then it came to me—this fellow was Leon Yater, the accountant that used to work . . ."

"Are you positive it was Mr. Yater?"

"Of course I'm positive." The old man seemed a bit miffed. "I reckon I know what I saw. My eyes ain't that bad yet."

"I'm sorry, Mr. Hansen," Phil said. "Then after you knew it was Leon Yater, what did you do?"

"I pulled over to the curb and stopped. Of course, I was on past him by that time, but I stopped and walked back. This Yater was standing in the middle of the sidewalk, watching me. I was as close to him as I am from that tree over there." Hansen stopped and pointed out a tree that stood in the next yard.

"That was close enough to recognize him," Phil said.

"You bet it was. I hollered to him. 'Hello there, Yater,' I yelled, and do you know what he did?"

"No," Phil said shortly.

"He disappeared. He ran right up the railroad track."

"Pardon me, Mr. Hansen," Phil said, "do you mean that spur railroad track that crosses First Street?"

"Is there any other?"

"Not that I know of, but I wanted to be sure. Which way did Yater run?"

"North," Hansen said with an emphatic nod of his head. "I didn't go after him. It's dark between those buildings, and I'm not as young as I once was. I didn't figure I had any chance of catching him anyway."

"Thank you for telling me this," Phil said. "I certainly appreciate your help." He told Hansen about the warrant served on his father in the hospital and his father's critical condition.

The old man's eyes blazed. "That's the finish as far as I'm concerned," he snapped. "If they did that to Carl Martinson, I'm through with the whole kit and caboodle of them. I'm marching down to city hall and I'm going to tell Tom Warford to his face what I think of his underhanded tricks."

"Mr. Hansen," Phil said soberly, "please don't do that. It wouldn't help my father one bit, and it would get you into trouble. You stay on your job and do your work as you have always done."

The old man looked back at the cottage behind him. "I suppose that's what I'll have to do," he said, shaking his head. "But a man can only put up with so much. Sometimes that gets to be too much."

"You've already done more than anyone else," Phil said. "I'll tell Dad as soon as—as he's better."

Phil drove back to First Street and parked by the railroad track where Hansen had seen Leon Yater. The district here was warehouses, with only a few persons around during the day. Phil could imagine it was completely deserted at night. He walked over and looked up the spur track to the north. He could see the boarded-up windows of Charters' feed and grain mill from here.

Beside the rear entrance to the Barnes Department Store, there was a dock for receiving and shipping merchandise. When Phil came up to the door, he saw a man sweeping off the dock. He asked the man if he had seen Bimbo Barnes around the store.

The man grinned broadly. "They put him to work in the stock room," he said with obvious delight. "I don't know whether old Grimsby will let you talk to him or not."

Phil found Bimbo alone, unpacking and stacking dishes. Bimbo looked up and glared when he saw Phil. "I told you," he groaned. "I told you, but you wouldn't listen." He wiped the beads of sweat from his round face and sighed deeply. "It happens every time."

"A little work won't kill you," Phil said without feeling. "It will melt some of that blubber off." Phil looked around. "Can you get away? I found out something important."

Bimbo straightened up, groaned, and grabbed his back. "Old Grimsby's around here someplace. He'd lay the whip to me if he caught me goofing off." He, too, looked around. "What did you find?" he asked.

Phil told him how Hansen had seen Leon Yater the night before. He explained about the spur railroad track, and how Yater had run toward the feed and grain mill. "What does that add up to?" Phil said.

Bimbo slapped his own leg. "It means Yater is hiding in that empty mill again," he said.

Phil nodded agreement. "He evidently wasn't in the cave when Warford's men went there. He slipped away and came back here to hide."

"His car is there," Bimbo said thoughtfully. "Maybe he intends to take off."

"He might have left last night after Hansen recognized him," Phil said. "I hope not, but I don't think he'd take a chance on leaving in daylight. If he didn't go last night, we've got all day to look for him."

A man's voice from inside the screened-in section yelled at Bimbo to get to work.

Bimbo grimaced. "That's Grimsby," he whispered. "I don't dare leave while he's here. But he takes a coffee break in a few minutes. I'll slip away then."

"I'm going over to the studio," Phil said in a low voice. "I still have some business with Scotty, so I'll meet you there.

Scotty looked up when Phil walked into the office. "Good morning," Scotty said. He hadn't made the remark sound sarcastic, and he didn't mention the time.

Phil had his speech well rehearsed. He intended to be businesslike and not mention anything personal. He had no proof against Scotty except what he had seen through the door the evening before. He didn't intend to say anything about the alligator shoes. Phil walked over and laid his key on the desk. "I'm afraid I'm going to have to quit," he said.

Scotty looked at the key. He leaned back in his chair and studied Phil. "I suppose you're doing what you think is best," he said. Then he went on before Phil could answer, "I'll hate to lose you, Phil. You were a good worker, and you would have made a good photographer."

"Thank you." Phil was glad Scotty hadn't asked him to explain why he was leaving. "You've taught me a lot." When Scotty was the way he was now, Phil felt almost ashamed of his suspicions. "I'll be pretty busy," he finished lamely.

Scotty nodded. The timer bell rang, and automatically, Phil started toward the darkroom. Scotty gave him a faint smile and came out of his chair. "I have some film in the tank. I'll take care of it."

Phil felt uncomfortable in the office now. He would have

gone outside to wait, but he knew he should say good-by to Scotty before he left. He was saved any further uneasiness when the door flew open and Bimbo burst in.

"Let's get over to Charters' mill," Bimbo said in spite of Phil's warning gestures. "Leon Yater is likely to pull out." Bimbo stopped and stared at Phil's frantic motions for silence. "Hey, what . . ."

Instead of trying to explain, Phil pushed Bimbo through the front door. He turned on him as soon as they were on the sidewalk. "You loudmouth," he growled, "Scotty was in the darkroom."

Bimbo stared at Phil, open-mouthed. "Why didn't you stop me?"

"I tried, but you wouldn't pay any attention."

Bimbo clapped his hand to the side of his head. "Ooooh," he groaned, "I just pulled the granddaddy of all the boo-boos."

"You sure did," Phil snapped. "Now Scotty knows Yater is supposed to be at Charters' mill. If Scotty really is King Rooster, Warford will have his men down there before we are."

Phil tried Charters' office door first, and when he found that locked, he led Bimbo around the building to the railroad track. The boxes were still there, so he piled them up and boosted the fat boy through the window. Bimbo was getting up from his hands and knees when Phil climbed into the room.

"Man, it's dirty in here," Bimbo said, brushing himself off.

Phil put his finger to his lips. "Shh," he warned, "we've got to be quiet." He listened, but there wasn't even the scurry of a rat. He tiptoed to the door and swung it open. He made sure nobody was outside before he led Bimbo out into the big room. "We'll make sure the car is here first," he whispered and headed for the stack of cartons.

They quietly pulled enough cartons back to reveal the old coupé underneath. "We're in luck," Bimbo whispered. "He's still here."

Phil pointed across the room to the short wooden platform. "I think that door up there leads to the front of the building. We'll try there first."

The boys climbed the three steps at the end of the platform and went through the door into a narrow, dark hall. At the end of the hall there was a cubicle with two more doors. Phil opened one and found himself in Charters' office. He looked around. Everything was the same as it had been on his other visits there.

Bimbo looked at the iron safe, the roll-top desk, and the rest of the furnishings. "Man, it's medieval," he said in an elaborate whisper. "All we need is a suit of armor standing in the corner."

Phil saw a door he hadn't noticed before. He walked over and opened it to find a closet with an old oilskin slicker hanging on a nail.

The boys went back down the narrow hall and stood on the platform. Phil studied the gloomy room for a possible hiding place. Bimbo shook his arm and pointed up across the room. The object Bimbo had indicated was a huge storage bin that ran up to the lofty ceiling. Phil supposed it had been filled with feed from the floor above, for the bottom part ended in a hopper, where trucks could be driven under it and filled.

High, near the top of the storage bin there was a narrow wooden catwalk, and Phil imagined there must be a ladder on the other side. He nodded, but he didn't really think the bin was worth investigating.

Phil led the way over to the room where he had found the machinery. Bimbo gaped at the huge iron monsters that stood neatly in a line, with only working space on either side.

Phil held Bimbo back as he studied the interior of the room. A shaft of light came through a window near the rear of the room. Phil stared at the one bright spot and saw tiny dust particles stirring around in the beam. The cloud was too heavy to have been raised by a rat—someone was in the room and had crossed the floor there recently.

Phil made sure that there was no other exit except the door behind them before he pulled Bimbo's ear close to his lips. "Yater is in this room," he whispered. "You go down that side of the machinery; I'll take the other side. If you see him, yell."

Bimbo nodded and started around the first machine. As soon as he disappeared, Phil began his search on the other side. He moved slowly, making certain he overlooked no space or cranny where a small man could hide himself.

Suddenly there was a fast clatter of running footsteps on the other side, then Bimbo's yell. "There he is!"

The footsteps were running on toward the back end of the room and Phil leaped ahead. He was in front of the last machine and running hard when a dark shadow darted out.

Phil leaped blindly through the air in a flying tackle, hit the man with his shoulder, and they rolled across the dusty floor together.

Phil struggled to untangle himself. Then he felt as if the roof had caved in on him, knocking him flat again. He raised up and looked back to see Bimbo sitting on top of them. "How did you like that tackle?" Bimbo asked.

"Get off of me, you moose." Phil got up and looked down on the other man, lying prostrate, his eyes glazed as he clutched at his throat. "You knocked the wind out of him," Phil said.

Bimbo bent over. "Is it Leon Yater?"

"It's Yater. Give me a hand." The boys pulled Yater to his feet and held him between them, although either boy could have done the job alone, with one hand.

Yater's sharp-featured little face was twisted in agony as he struggled to fill his lungs with air. When he raised his head, his pointed nose made Phil think of a weasel. "You shouldn't have run," Phil told him. "We're friends of Virgil Charters."

Yater shook himself and the color began to flow back into his face. He gasped a few times. "All we wanted was those records," Bimbo said.

Yater waggled his head back and forth, then managed to speak. "Everybody wants them," he said weakly.

"Not as badly as we do," Phil said tersely.

Yater twisted his face around to look up at Phil. "How much you willing to pay then?"

Phil stared at him in shocked silence. "We're not going to pay anything," Bimbo said.

Yater struggled. The man had surprising strength and had almost twisted away when Phil grabbed him and threw on an arm lock. "Leave me alone," Yater whined. "You're breaking my arm."

"I'll break your neck. Now what do you mean, how much are we going to pay you for those records?"

"Did Charters offer to buy them?" Bimbo demanded.

"He offered them to Charters if Charters would hide him. Then he welshed on the deal," Phil said angrily.

Yater didn't deny the charge. "They're mine," he said defiantly.

Phil knew all this was useless bickering. It had been a blow when he realized that Yater had taken the records only for the purpose of selling them to the highest bidder. "You called my father on the phone," he said tersely. "You told him to meet you at the cemetery. Did you intend to try to sell him those records?"

Yater pulled back his lips. His front teeth showed. It made him look more like a weasel than ever, Phil thought. "Those records would have meant more to your father than to anybody else, except Warford."

"Why didn't you meet him then?"

Yater spat on the floor. "Some guy with a big dog scared me off. I never got another chance." Yater looked up sideways. "Those records are worth a lot of money to the right guys."

Phil thought of his father lying near death in the hospital. He wanted to smash this little rat in the face. He wanted to beat him until Yater would be glad to tell him where the records were. Instead, he put pressure on the arm lock and made Yater wince, but that gave Phil small satisfaction. He applied more pressure and Yater yelped in agony as his legs buckled under him. "Turn loose," Yater cried, "turn loose and I'll tell you something."

Phil loosened his hold and let the little man straighten up. "This had better be good," he said.

"You want to know about King Rooster, don't you? I know who he is." Phil released his hold, and Yater nodded. "I made a lot of entries in those records of payments to King Rooster. That was what Warford always called him, but he never told anybody who King Rooster was. But I know now," Yater said slyly.

"All right," Phil snapped. "Who is King Rooster?"

Yater started to pull away, and Phil slapped the arm lock on again. "Don't," Yater groaned, "I'm going to show you something."

Phil grabbed one arm while Bimbo took the other. Yater led them back up on the platform and through the hall to the cubicle. "What are you trying to pull?" Bimbo said.

"Yesterday I found these calendars up here on the wall," Yater said, reaching up to finger through a stack.

Phil swung the office door open to let some light into the cubicle. He saw the date on the top calendar was for eleven years before, and that it bore an advertisement for the Charters Feed and Grain Company. As Yater lifted the calendars, Phil saw they had been hung there in chronological order, one year on top of the year before.

The boys watched as Yater lifted one after another, until he stopped at a calendar for the year sixteen years before. Phil stared at the advertisement. It was of a big rooster in full color. The rooster wore a gold crown and the lettering underneath said,

KING ROOSTER
CHARTERS ROYAL POULTRY FEED

"Virgil Charters is King Rooster?" Phil said, not believing what he saw.

"That's right," a quiet voice said from behind them.

Phil turned to see Charters standing in the open office doorway, his face hard and a stubby revolver held in his hand. "That 'King Rooster' was a private joke of Warford's. He was one of my dealers up north, and he always thought that name was funny."

The two boys and Yater were jammed into the cubicle, so Charters' gun covered them all.

"You knew Tom Warford before he was mayor?" Bimbo asked.

"A long time before. He was always a smart man, so when the mill closed down, I brought him in and made him mayor of Seacrest. Nobody knew he called me King Rooster except Yater there."

"We did," Bimbo said. "It was on that tape recording we had of Warford's voice."

Charters frowned. "I didn't know that. Lucky I erased that tape."

Leon Yater had cowered back against the wall. He seemed to regain some of his nerve as he pointed a shaking forefinger at Charters. "Warford threw you over," he said. "He kicked you out. He told me a couple of weeks ago that there wouldn't be any more payments to King Rooster, that he was going to do without him."

"Tom Warford is a fool."

Phil's eyes were on the gun, not on Charters' face. His mind worked furiously, trying to straighten out the sudden change of events. "Was that why Warford's men tried to kidnap you on Ramona Road?" he asked.

Yater spoke before Charters could answer. "Charters intended to doublecross me," he said. "He was going to sell my records back to Warford on his own hook. When I wouldn't give them to him, he couldn't deliver. Warford was desperate and decided to take them away from Charters."

"Man," Bimbo said, "everybody down at city hall was doublecrossing everybody else. I guess my father finally caught onto you."

Charters snorted. "I had Samuel Barnes fooled. It was that Melton Flood who got suspicious." He waved the gun impatiently. "I'm through playing games. I want those records, Yater."

Yater's body trembled violently. "You'll never get them," he whimpered. "I won't tell you where they are."

The benevolent mask Charters had worn was now ripped away, revealing an evil copy of his former face. His eyes were steely hard, and Phil felt he could look through them and back into Charters' brain. What he saw made him sick, for it was a mind so twisted by the craving for money and power that there was no reasoning left.

"I'll run Tom Warford out of town with those records," Charters said, breathing heavily. "I'm going to take over then."

"You'll never take over this town," Yater said, pulling himself up to face Charters. "I fixed that. I found your own set of books here. I went through them, and there's enough there to send you up for ten years."

Phil looked over at the row of very old ledgers in the bookcase. He stared at them. There was something wrong, something he couldn't put his finger on. His attention was pulled away from the ledgers when Charters backed toward his roll-top desk.

Yater burst out with a cackling laugh. "You won't find your books in there," he said. "I took them. I took them and hid them where you'll never find them." He laughed again. "You tried to doublecross me—nobody doublecrosses Leon Yater. I got even. I wrote Warford a note yesterday. I told him where your books were, and he'll send you to jail, Charters. I'm going to turn your books over to Warford. He'll bust you, King Rooster—he'll bust you into nothing."

Phil realized that he and Bimbo were trapped with two maniacs instead of one. The men were so intent on their struggle with each other that they paid no attention to the boys. Phil couldn't run away because Bimbo was jammed between Yater and the wall. He couldn't leave Bimbo alone.

Yater shook with unreasoning laughter. "I hid them!" he shrieked. "I hid my records—your books, everything, right here under your nose. But you'll never find them, Charters. You'll never find them, King Rooster."

"Don't call me that," Charters yelled back. For a moment he hesitated beside his desk. The gun in his hand wavered as he reached toward a drawer with the other hand.

Yater took that chance to break and run down the hall.

Phil dropped to the floor, expecting a shot. Instead, Charters ran past Phil without hesitating and on down the hall toward the big room.

"We've got to get help," Bimbo gasped, coming to his feet. "I'll call my father."

Phil shook his head and grabbed Bimbo's arm. Thoughts were whirling through his mind so fast that it was impossible to sort them out. Samuel Barnes wasn't their answer. Then he remembered Charters' words. "Call Melton Flood," he said. "Tell him what's happened here."

Bimbo started for the phone, then turned. "Where are you going?"

"I'm going to try and stop Charters before he kills somebody."

Bimbo grabbed the telephone. "I'll be out to help you as soon as I call," he said.

Phil was halfway down the hall when he heard the shot from the big room. He stopped at the door and saw Charters in the center of the room, his gun still pointed upward. Phil followed the pointed gun with his eyes and saw Yater on the catwalk, high on the storage bin. Yater had been hit. He staggered backward, flailing his arms in the air. He struck the railing and toppled over, and his body fell in a slow arc, turning over once in mid-air before it struck the wooden floor.

Charters ran to Yater's body and leaned over. "You were the same kind of a fool Tom Warford is," he said in a flat voice. "Nobody is going to stop Virgil Charters."

Phil took the opportunity to slip down the steps and get around the pile of grain bags. He stayed close to the wall in the shadows while he searched for a weapon. Somehow he had to disarm Charters. Phil dropped down beside the heap of cartons that covered Yater's car. When Charters turned his head, Phil wriggled back out of sight.

The big room was so quiet that Charters' voice sounded loud, although he spoke in a low tone. "You lost, Yater," he said. "Warford will never get my books. Nobody will ever get them." Charters dropped the gun into his coat pocket and hurried over to the wall beside the grain bags, where a steel drum lay on its side, supported on a wooden rack. Charters turned the spigot at the end and a stream of oil flowed out. Charters grabbed an arm load of the grain bags and dumped them under the oil stream.

Phil realized that he had put himself in a spot. Charters was working between him and the platform, and at any moment Bimbo might appear in the doorway. Charters seemed to have forgotten the boys for the moment, but Phil knew once Charters saw Bimbo, nothing would stop him. Phil braced himself to attract Charters' attention at the first movement in the doorway.

Charters was working frantically now. He would fill a bucket with oil, and while the stream was still running over the bags, he rushed across and dashed the oil over the wooden platform and steps. Phil knew what Charters intended to do, but he was powerless to stop him. Phil thought of the room behind him with the broken window. He could slip back there and escape, but there was still Bimbo in the office.

Charters was sloshing the walls with oil now. The mill was a frame building. The wood was old and dry, and once a blaze took hold in the barnlike structure, it would be a roaring inferno within minutes.

Phil stared fascinated at the oil spreading out across the floor, being sucked up by the porous wood. He judged the open space between him and Charters. He thought of the gun in Charters' pocket and how the crazed man hadn't hesitated to shoot Yater down. Phil remembered Bimbo's promise to come out as soon as he had made the call to Melton Flood. Phil groaned at his own helplessness.

CHAPTER 17

THE BIG DRUM must have been well filled, for the oil still streamed out as Charters carried soaked grain bags over and placed them under the platform and along the walls. Phil had to restrain himself to keep from yelling when he saw Charters light a match. Once that blaze started, the records that would save his father's life would be destroyed forever.

The flame flickered, and when it grew, Charters dropped it on the bags on the floor. As each bag caught fire, he would grab it by the end and hurl it against the platform and the walls.

The flames leaped and spread across the oil-soaked dry wood. Thick black smoke rolled up the walls in billows. The murky interior of the big room was dotted by leaping sheets of flame.

Charters looked around him and laughed. He started for the platform. Then Phil saw him freeze and claw in his pocket for his gun. Bimbo, Phil thought, and threw the cartons aside to rush Charters. He stopped when he saw the figure on the platform was not Bimbo, but the tall plainclothesman who had taken him to Warford's office. Charters whirled and ran toward the rear of the mill.

The tall man's partner appeared and fired a shot before both men jumped down from the platform and ran after Charters.

Phil ran back across the room. He had no idea whether more of Warford's men were in the office, but he knew he had to get to Bimbo. Sounds of crackling fire filled the air, and the room was lighted with a red glow when Phil reached the platform. Charters had thrown oil down the hall, and flames crept along the floor.

The double doors were held closed by a long wooden bar placed in slots at either end and in the middle. Phil heaved up on the bar, but it refused to budge. He ran down and found the end fastened with a padlock.

Phil estimated the height of the platform. It wasn't much taller than the high hurdles he had run in school, but here he would have to land in a sheet of flame. On beyond that there was the smoke and flame-choked hall to pass through.

He judged the distance to the front edge of the platform and knelt into starting position. He took a deep breath, jumped forward, and paced his strides so that he would be on his right foot when he was the proper distance from the platform. When his foot struck the floor, Phil put everything he had into his leap.

He struck the platform floor and went to his knees, scrambled up, and dived through the door. He charged down the hall, feeling his way, and with his lungs ready to burst for the want of air. Dizziness struck him as he reached the cubicle and he groped wildly until he found the door knob. He twisted, and pitched forward into the clear air of

Charters' office. Forcing himself to his knees, Phil looked around. The office was empty—Bimbo was not here.

Phil grasped the handle on the closet door to pull himself up, and the door swung open. Inside he saw Bimbo's body jammed into the narrow space.

Dizziness struck Phil again. He leaned over to tug at Bimbo's arm, but he could scarcely budge that, let alone move the entire body. Smoke was curling up from the crack beneath the door and panic hit Phil, making him clutch wildly at Bimbo's jacket.

A pair of hands pulled Phil away, and in his daze Phil thought he saw a man bend over Bimbo's body. Another man joined the first, and together they worked Bimbo out and carried him through the front door. The men laid the body on the sidewalk, and as he sank to the curb, Phil saw that the man who was bending over Bimbo was Scotty Kendall.

Phil's head had cleared some when Scotty stood up. "Bimbo's all right," he said. "He's got a nasty bump, but he'll come around."

"Warford's men did it," Phil said. "A couple of plainclothesmen." He tried to collect his thoughts. There was something important he was supposed to know—something he *had* to do. He turned to stare at the smoke pouring from the office door. He could see the flames inside, but turned back when he heard Bimbo moan.

Bimbo slowly opened his eyes. "Ohh," he groaned. He sat up and tried to get to his feet, but Scotty pushed him back. Bimbo looked at Phil, then over at the building. "The place is on fire," he said dully.

"Those two guys who held us in the civic auditorium hit you," Phil said.

Bimbo rubbed the knot on his head. "I remember—the short guy came through the office with a gun. I started to follow him, then . . ."

"The other one must have clobbered you from behind." Phil pushed himself to his feet. He felt much better now. The dizziness was gone in the fresh air, and he was beginning to remember things. "Warford's men chased Charters," he told Scotty. "Maybe they shot him."

Scotty shook his head. "They didn't shoot him," he said. "We had the rear door covered. Charters is being held under protective custody."

Phil stared. "We?" he said, bewildered. "Who put him under protective custody?"

Scotty grinned and stepped to one side to show the other man, who had remained in the background. "This is Ed Newman," he said. "He's from the Bureau of Internal Revenue."

Bimbo struggled up. "The federal government?" he asked in an awed voice.

Scotty nodded. "They've been working on the case for some time now. I've been doing what I could to help them. You can rob a town blind, but when you don't pay income tax on what you've stolen, you're in trouble with the federal government."

Phil bowed his head and stared at the ground behind Scotty. "Look, Bimbo!" he yelled. "Alligator shoes!"

Ed Newman looked embarrassed. "My brother-in-law is a

shoe salesman," he said. "These were a sample pair. They fit me, so he gave them to me."

"What's this about shoes?" Scotty said.

"I'll explain later." Phil rapped his head with his knuckles to stir up his memory. Was it something he had seen—or heard . . . ?

"We weren't ready to move in yet," Ed Newman said, "but when Scotty Kendall called and told me Leon Yater might be here in the mill, we had to act. We'd heard Yater had some records we had to have for evidence."

"Yater's records," Phil said. "That's it, Yater's records!" He turned and ran back through the door. Flames were eating the varnish away along the top of the railing. The door to the cubicle was burned away and the fire had crossed the floor and was climbing up the side of the bookcase. The backs of the old ledgers were hot to Phil's fingers. He was too blinded by smoke to see now, so he had to feel over three books from the left. He pulled the heavy ledger out and with it held close against his body, he groped his way back out through the front door.

Tears streamed down his face as he handed the ledger over to Ed Newman. "If I was right, this should give you a good case against both Virgil Charters and Mayor Warford."

Phil rubbed his eyes as Ed Newman opened the ledger. "Look at this," Newman said. "Somebody has cut out a lot of the old yellowed pages and put in new ones."

Phil grinned to himself. He had been right. He had finally remembered what was troubling him: when Yater told Charters he had found Charters' set of books, Phil had thought at first that he meant the ancient ledgers in the

bookcase. What Phil had noticed at the time and had remembered now was that *only one* of the ledgers was not covered with dust.

Yater had bragged that he had hidden the books under
Charters' nose, and to Phil that meant they were still in the
office. What better hiding place could there be than an old,
out-dated ledger of a company that had been out of business
for ten years?

"I wish somebody would tell me what's going on," Bimbo
said.

Phil grinned. "I'll explain it all over a malt sometime. He
heard the siren of the fire apparatus coming down First
Street. "It will be a waste of water trying to save this place,"
he said. "It's about ready to collapse. Let's move back before
it falls on us."

Ed Newman still studied the ledger as they walked across
the street. Finally he closed the book and put it under his
arm. "This seems to be just what we were looking for," he
said to Phil. "Thanks to you, I think we'll have a good, solid
income tax evasion case against both Mayor Warford and
Virgil Charters."

Scotty bunched his eyebrows. "It was just a case of getting
the right dogs on the quarry," he said and gave Phil a cynical grin. "I hope you don't mind me calling you one of the
dogs, Phil."

"I don't care what you call me, just as long as they stick
Warford and Charters."

"They will," Scotty said, "and with Warford in prison,
maybe some of the citizens will wake up and put a decent
administration into office." He looked over at Phil with a

serious expression. "You won't have to worry about your father. I think that from now on, they're going to start to appreciate Carl Martinson around Seacrest."

Later in the malt shop, Bimbo looked at Phil over a concoction of ice cream, fruit, and whipped cream. "I need it," he said. "It's brain food, and I've been under a strain."

"With your brain, you should have ordered a half portion," Phil said and settled back. He felt great. When he had talked to Dr. Calvin, he had been told that his news was better than anything a doctor could do to help his father.

"How did the internal revenue men get interested in Warford and Charters?" Bimbo asked.

"Scotty got in touch with them. When he saw the Citizens' Protective League could never get the job done, he called in the federal government."

"Good old Scotty," Bimbo said.

"When I'm sure Dad is on the mend, I'd like to take a couple of days off," Phil said. "How about a fishing trip next week?"

Bimbo shook his head. "I can't," he said sadly. "I have to go down to Los Angeles and fix things up to enter college this fall." He dropped his spoon and a blob of ice cream hit him in the nose. "Hey," he yelled, "why don't you go down with me?"

Phil grinned broadly. "I can't think of a single reason in the world why not," he said.

Date Due